ALICE

Written by Avalon Roselin
Illustrated by R. Hamlin

Roselin Books

Roselin Books
California
www.roselinbooks.com

Book Layout © 2014 BookDesignTemplates.com

ALiCE/ Avalon Roselin. – anniversary ed.
ISBN: 978-0-9976479-8-3

Visit us at www.roselinbooks.com

Content Warnings:
Ableism, Abuse, Alcohol Use, Brief Adult Language, Cannibalism, Character Death, Child Abuse, Disturbing Imagery, Gore, Implied Eating Disorder, Implied Self Harm, Medical Trauma, Mental Health/Mental Illness, Mention of Drug Use, Psychological Manipulation/Gaslighting, Sexual Assault/Rape (Non-Graphic), Suicidal Ideation, Suicide, Trauma, Violence, Vomiting

For Reye,
Who brought this nightmare into the waking world

With Special Thanks to:
M. Boucher, T. Pilgrim,
C. Conway, K. B. Cook, F. Fleecy, A. Pear, A. Weiss

I wish you the most wondrous of nightmares.

CHAPTER ONE

*A**ppearances can be deceiving.*
This fact is well known to anyone who has ever spent a night awake staring down a menacing shadow, only for the morning light to reveal the source of terror to be a child's toy or a tree branch.

If one were to look at Woodrow Children's Asylum, the overall impression would be one of despair. The asylum, located conveniently in the middle of nowhere, was an old brick building with ivy clinging to its walls. Like every other form of life around the dreary place, the ivy had long since dried into withered, brown tendrils, desperately grasping the building—almost as if to drag the asylum down into the grave with it. Neither birds nor crickets chirped, and there were never any cars in the driveway other than the old, rusty Volkswagen that belonged to the woman in charge of the asylum. If a stranger were to happen upon the place, they would either feel completely alone and isolated from society or that they were in the company of ghosts.

If this stranger were to go inside, they would find their suspicions largely confirmed. The asylum was haunted not by ghosts, but by dreary-looking children, a rather large old woman who called herself Madam Margot, and a young man named Christopher Robinson.

Madam Margot was in charge of the asylum, though rarely seen. She spent most of her time in her office reading romance novels and occasionally sorting out paperwork. Once every other blue moon, she met with people interested in adopting one of the children and made arrangements for them, which was odd, because children disappeared from the asylum far more frequently than new parents appeared.

Christopher saw to the daily needs of the children. In addition to dispensing food, water, and medicine, he also dispensed what the children needed most: care and attention. He worked without stopping to make sure that each child had a chance at positive human interaction, rising at dawn each day and toiling nearly until sunrise came again. With all the day's work falling to him, he hardly ever had time to accomplish all that he meant to do, such as clean the dingy windows to let some light in. The long days spent without sunlight had paled his skin to white and darkened his hair to black.

That particular morning, Christopher woke just as the sun was beginning to rise. He only knew it because the window in his room would not close all the way, leaving him a small opening through which to glance at the outside world.

Thankfully, the asylum wasn't at its full capacity of thirty residents, which gave Christopher a little more time to spend with each of the children as he made the rounds, starting at the first room in the East Wing.

The East Wing contained six bedrooms with two bunk beds each for the children. Christopher's room, one empty guest bedroom, and many operational rooms like the kitchen and washroom were located in the North Wing. Madam Margot's office and room was by itself in the South Wing.

The morning disarray in the East Wing was just what he expected. After all, he had been in charge of assigning the rooms, and did so based on behavior and any problems the children had. The first room's occupants, Malcolm and Jenna, were the youngest children in the asylum and had bed-wetting issues, so he'd placed them closest to the washroom to cut a few seconds out of his daily walk with arms full of sheets.

Next came Caitlin, Thea, and Jennifer, who were shy and generally withdrawn but otherwise healthy by Woodrow standards. Christopher was careful in waking them so they didn't startle, and they got to work making their own beds and talking quietly to each other about the previous night's dreams. It was encouraging to see what good friends they had become over the months, and Christopher hoped they would be placed in homes together or with other children who had similar dispositions.

The third room belonged to Thomas and Joshua, who were even more easily startled than the girls, and who often had more serious issues than simply being withdrawn. Thomas had thrown up at some time during the night, and Christopher cleaned it up while assuring both of the sobbing children that it wasn't their fault. He would include some-thing to soothe Thomas's nervous stomach with breakfast, if there was anything in the asylum that could do that. Of course there wasn't, but Christopher held onto the hope that there might be, no matter how many times he was disap-pointed by the bare cupboards.

The next room was always a mess, but not one that required much cleaning on Christopher's part. Anderson, Ray, and Sarah were the hyperactive children of the asylum, and their room always looked like a storm had blown through it. They were already awake by the time he arrived, of course, too excited to sleep in (and, the caretaker was very sure, two of the three were probably insomniacs). His morn-ing greeting to them always included a light scolding, and they would start making their beds and cleaning their room only to get distracted and never finish.

The fifth room was one that Christopher always dreaded. These were the violent children, the ones who hit and bit and screamed at the least provocation, if any. He felt guilty about his dislike of them and was very sure that they were really sweet boys deep down. He knew it wasn't their fault. What he didn't know was what he could do for them; the only thing that seemed to settle them was their medicine, and that had to be administered at such high doses that they were relatively unresponsive for the rest of the day, so therapy wasn't much good. Christopher had tried therapy without medicating them. It had ended with a black eye and several bites that needed disinfecting.

The second he opened the door he was met with loud shrieking. He gave each of the four boys a quick check. They were tied down to their beds to prevent them from hurting themselves or each other during the night. Freddy was the one who was screaming, but he was alright. Mike was as silent as ever, and both Jed and Jason's self-inflicted scratches were healing nicely with no evidence of more being added overnight. Christopher left as soon as he was done. He would undo the straps later when he had given them their medicine and something to eat.

The next room was always much quieter and more pleasant. This one contained the only siblings at the asylum: Alice, Lorina, and Edith. They took care of each other most of the time and left Christopher with little work to do for them, as they didn't require medicine. Aside from the fact that they were orphans, they were completely normal little girls, even if they did play make-believe a little too often and with a little too much fervor. They were already having a pretend tea party when Christopher arrived, and he left them to it, being just a bit too busy at the moment to participate but promising he'd stay for the next one.

Finally, he made his way down the West Wing, to its one inhabitant.

This child, Mickey Walters, was an unusual case even for Woodrow Children's Asylum. Christopher never liked putting any of the children alone and was absolutely loath to have placed one in a room so far away from the others, but he hadn't seen any other choice. Mickey didn't have any problems with bedwetting or nervous vomiting, and no behavioral problems as far as Christopher could tell, but he didn't get along with any of the others. The shy girls hid whenever he was around; the violent boys would always start yelling and destroying whatever was in reach—whether they were medicated or not—if they so much as saw him; the hyperactive trio would stop whatever they were doing and be perfectly still if he was in the same room as them; the sisters outright refused to acknowledge Mickey's existence.

Most of the doors in the West Wing were sealed. The ones that had been covered were once again visible as the rotting wallpaper peeled away. Christopher didn't mind it. He had always hated the ugly yellow color Madam Margot had picked for this section of the asylum. However, the cracked drywall beneath wasn't exactly attractive.

Christopher reached the little door at the end of the corridor. It always struck him as odd that the door was shorter than the rest, as if the hallway had slanted downward about a foot—which, of course, it hadn't, but the West Wing seemed to be fond of such optical illusions.

Nevertheless, the young man turned the doorknob and stepped into the room with the boy.

Mickey was, like all the inhabitants of the asylum, thin and pale. His mop of dead-leaf-brown hair was forever out of place and tangled, though Mickey himself was always clean and proper. Two clever hazel eyes peered out at Christopher with the disturbing gaze of someone who knew far more than they should and was keeping secrets. They were softened only by the contemplative, if not somewhat sad, upturning of lips that just barely passed for a smile.

"Hello, Christopher."

"Hello, Mickey. How are you feeling today?"

"No better or worse than yesterday, but... different."

"Different? How so?"

The boy chewed on his lower lip for a moment and shook his head.

"Well then. What are we going to do about this?" Christopher asked, dropping onto the bed next to Mickey, causing the lumpy mattress to bounce up and down.

"Christopher—don't," Mickey said in the all-too-serious tone children sometimes use.

"I could go get some medicine..."

"Christopher—"

"Or some more crackers..."

"I mean it, don't you dare!"

"Or..."

"Christopher!"

And at this, Christopher turned and tickled the boy's midsection with swift, experienced fingers. Normally the boy's face would light up in a fit of laughter while he squirmed and protested too much. His giddy giggling would likewise plaster a smile on Christopher's face, and in a minute it would end with both of them in higher spirits.

But Mickey did none of those things. His body remained still and stiff and his gaze fixed on Christopher without the slightest hint of amusement. If anything he looked more troubled than before, now frowning.

For a painful second Christopher's heart missed a beat. "What's wrong?"

Mickey kept his mouth closed stubbornly.

"Mickey, please tell me what's wrong. I can't help you if you don't."

"You're going to leave."

"Well, of course. I have work to do, but I have a few minutes to spare if you need to talk to me." Was it loneliness, then, that had caused Mickey's dark mood? "Maybe it would help things if you left this room and interacted with some of the other children so you wouldn't be too lonely while I'm working. Would you like that?"

"No. They all hate me."

"That isn't true. You haven't really had a chance to get acquainted with them. They're shy too, you know, but I'm very sure that if you were around a little more they'd get used to you."

Mickey narrowed his eyes. "You know that none of what you just said is the least bit accurate. You've seen how they act around me. You know I'm different. You just don't want to acknowledge it because you don't want to admit that there's nothing you can do to help me. You don't even know what's wrong with me."

The orderly stared at the boy in shock. Mickey had never spoken to him this way before, and it hurt. He knew Mickey was antisocial, but he'd always assumed that they shared something of a special bond. Of course, Christopher knew friendship alone wasn't enough to solve all or any of Mickey's problems, but it still bothered him to think that he might have unintentionally done something to put distance between them.

"I... well," Christopher said, trying to gather his thoughts. "Being different doesn't mean you shouldn't make friends. And you're right, I don't know what to do to help you. I'm not even sure there's anything 'wrong' with you in the first place. But I *am* making my best effort, and I would like it if you would try, too."

"It's pointless." Mickey curled his knees up to his chest and rested his chin on them. "You're going to leave."

This piqued Christopher's interest, being the second time Mickey had said that. He was at the asylum, after all; maybe he had abandonment issues and was acting out because he thought Christopher was going to stop paying attention to him. "This isn't *just* about my work, is it?"

Mickey laughed, but it was cold. "No. This isn't just about your work."

"I don't understand, Mickey. What do you mean by 'leaving'?"

The boy grew quiet again.

"Do you mean... dying?" Christopher was morbidly relieved at the direction the conversation had taken. He had seen abandonment issues before, and there were far, far worse things that could affect a child than losing a family member too soon.

Mickey's shoulders shook a little, and it didn't take more than a second or two for Christopher to recognize the telltale signs of crying. Usually Mickey was calm, even unemotional in a way that was unnerving in a child, which was something that always caused Christopher to worry. For him to be crying in front of someone else, even if he was trying to hide it, something must be deeply wrong.

Christopher wrapped his arms around the boy's shivering frame and brought him close. To his relief Mickey didn't pull away, instead choosing to lean into Christopher's comforting embrace.

"Shh, now. It's okay. I'm sorry for bringing it up."

"No. It isn't what you think."

"Oh?"

"You think I'm crying because you mentioned death, and that my parents died or something."

Christopher was glad that Mickey was more or less buried in his sweater so he couldn't see the look of shock on his face at that moment.

He brushed it off. Mickey was an intelligent child; surely he had guessed Christopher's train of thought. Thankfully he went on before Christopher had to think about it too much.

"I'm crying because I'm frustrated that you don't understand, and I don't know how to phrase it to make you understand. It's a normal thing to be sad about."

That was mildly offensive, but Christopher chose to ignore it. "What is it that I don't understand? And even if you're having a hard time putting it into words, it might be a good idea to try to explain it anyway. I'll never understand if you don't try to tell me, and talking it through might help you find the right way to say it."

"You wouldn't believe me if I did."

"How do you know?"

"I know because I know you. A lot better than you think, actually."

Christopher wasn't sure how much more of this kind of talk he could withstand—it certainly wasn't flattering—but he didn't want to hurt Mickey's feelings. His own comfort would need to be put aside for the moment. Mickey certainly felt that whatever message he was trying to get across was important.

Mickey's stare pierced him. "Do you think I'm crazy?"

"No."

"Do you trust me?"

Christopher hesitated. "Yes."

"Good. Just remember that and listen to what I say." Mickey sighed and wiped his eyes, not that it did much good. "Please, Christopher. I can't tell you much, but you have to listen when I do."

They sat in silence for longer than they should have. Although Christopher did not feel right leaving him alone to cry, there was nothing he could do for Mickey, and he was behind schedule as it was. He patted the boy's shoulder and kissed his forehead; then out of the room and back down the hall he went.

However, the hall seemed different this time, as if the walls had grown eyes. Christopher shivered under their intense, depraved gaze, hurried and haunted by the image of all those imagined pupils following his movements. The feeling wasn't foreign; he often felt as if some unknown force was watching him. No matter how many times he experienced it, it never ceased to alarm him.

He shuffled out of the hall and into a startled Madam Margot, who for once had left her office to attend to her responsibilities.

"Christopher! What in heaven's name are you doing?"

"I-I was just... uh..."

Christopher looked over his shoulder into the hall. As always, there was nothing there. Nothing but a musty old hall in a musty old building.

Except...

At its end was a table with a vase, in which there were dried, browning plants that might have been beautiful flowers once upon a time, standing in place of the door to Mickey's room. Christopher shook his head. His eyes had to be playing tricks on him. There had never been any vase in the West Wing, but no matter how he rubbed his eyes or squinted the vase remained and the door was gone.

Madam Margot snatched his arm to get his attention. He immediately jerked back, but she had accomplished her goal. "Now don't you start acting up! I don't need another crazy person to wait on. Get back to work. If you've got time to be poking around old halls, you've got time to be useful! There might be some potential buyers—"

"Adopters, you mean?"

"—coming by later this evening. I want this place spotless. You've been lazy enough, letting it get this bad in the first place, so it makes sense to me that you should be the one to clean it up. Now get to it!"

He nodded. "Y-yes, Madam."

As she walked away, he glanced once more into the hall. Still empty, still no door at the end. He would have gone in to investigate, but there was a sudden breath on the back of his neck, and he could feel a laughing pair of eyes on him, looming over the vase, drowning out the sobs of a child.

He hurried away and shook his head back and forth once more as he did. He must have just inhaled some kind of mold spore that didn't agree with him. Of course there was a door at the end of the hall; how could he have gotten into Mickey's room otherwise? He hadn't spent the past several minutes talking to no one.

It warranted further investigation, but Christopher was far too rattled to do it that minute.

The rest of the day's hours came and went without any oddities for Madam Margot or the children, and Christopher was kept far too busy dusting, scrubbing the floors, and trying for the hundredth time to get stains out of the furniture to think too much about what had happened in the West Wing earlier.

He was sore and his fingers felt like they'd start bleeding any second, but he managed to clean all of the rooms that any potential adopters would see. There was no time to rest or congratulate himself on that, though; dinner had to be made at once. All they had was a weak, watery soup made with undercooked cabbage and overcooked carrots, but it was better than starving.

The children were glad to have their supper, and when they finished eating Christopher settled them in with a movie while he worked up the courage to go back to the West Wing to give Mickey his meal. He had put it off for long enough. Besides, he knew what was real and what wasn't, and no one in their right mind would bother sneaking into the orphanage just to torment some orderly who didn't have a cent to his name.

Unfortunately, the door at the end of the hall still wasn't there. And the other doors in the hallway weren't where they were supposed to be.

They were in the walls of the hallway, yes, but they were in *all* the walls. Doors of all sizes stood within the sides, ceiling, and floor of the corridor.

Some of them were covered in police tape.

Others were oozing blood.

The dim lighting did nothing to help Christopher's courage, and he turned around only to find that, instead of the open entryway that should have been behind him, there loomed a black wall with a single door. Where the eyehole would be, there was instead a staring, bloodshot eye.

The soup bowl shattered on the doorknob at Christopher's feet as he scrambled backwards and stumbled over another doorframe. One of his hands struck the door under him and pushed it open, sending him falling through it and into darkness...

♥ 12 ♦

"CHRISTOPHER!"

The young man sat up with a jolt at the sudden loud noise, which he did not register as his name until a few seconds passed. Madam Margot stood over him with a disapproving leer in her eyes that was brought to heart-stopping heights by the flashlight in her hand.

Christopher looked around; the soup bowl was in pieces and the hallway was just as it ever was. The door at the end slowly became visible as his eyes adjusted to the dark.

"Oh, I'm sorry!"

"I can't say I care all that much. Just make sure this mess is cleaned up. After that, there are some things that need to be picked up from town, and the power's out."

"Why is the power—" A loud crash of thunder both interrupted and answered him. "Never mind."

"I'm going to bed. No point staying up in this nasty weather, can't even read my romances and I doubt anyone would be foolish enough to be out in this storm." She handed him a strip of paper. "Here's the list. Off to work, now."

"Are the children in bed yet?"

"Why would I know that? You're the one who deals with them," she said with a roll of her eyes. "Just get this taken care of!"

"Yes, Madam."

As she stalked away, Christopher knelt down and began picking up the shattered pieces of the bowl as well as he could in the dark. It occurred to him that if he had fainted there, for whatever reason, Mickey had never gotten his dinner.

Unfortunately, Christopher didn't have the nerve to go further into the West Wing. He knew Mickey could put himself to bed just fine with or without supper. He only hoped that the boy didn't think he was being punished for their earlier conversation.

Christopher checked the recreation room first and found it empty. The East Wing was quiet. When he looked in on each room, the beds were properly occupied. Jason, Jed, Mike, and Freddy were even secure in their bunks and sleeping soundly. He couldn't imagine that Madam Margot had done this, nor would he have wanted her to.

Had he taken care of everything while he'd been blacked out, and simply forgotten?

In any case, the children had been attended to and he had other chores waiting. He went to the kitchen and found a flashlight with which to read the list. As he scanned the list, he realized they were out of absolutely everything. Food, medicine, toilet paper, *everything*. The food could wait until morning, and the toilet paper too, but the medicine was too important.

With a new sense of urgency, Christopher swiped the keys to the Volkswagen, opened the front door, and stepped out into the wind and rain. He rushed to the car, got inside, and turned it on, nearly freezing in the process as his clothes were drenched by the frigid downpour. He wouldn't be surprised in the least if the rain turned to hail. He turned on the heater as soon as his shaking fingers would allow only to remember that the heater hadn't worked in over a year.

The car was slow with age and neglect. Christopher had never once seen Madam Margot drive—he didn't even know if she had a license or not—so the car was only driven once a month when he made a run to town for supplies.

It was at that moment that Christopher realized Madam Margot hadn't given him any money for supplies. He could just imagine what would happen if he tried to go back and ask her now. She would sneer at him and say, "Have you forgotten how to make money?"

Christopher applied gentle pressure to the gas pedal and the car clanked down the road that wound its way around the cliffs, rocked by the storm and uneven surface. In the glare of the headlights Christopher could make out the swaying figures of the trees, their branches whipping back and forth, almost like people who would run out into the road and wave their arms to stop drivers from potentially

hitting a cat or to warn of dangers like the bridge ahead being out.

The thought sent a chill up Christopher's spine, and
he pressed the pedal a little harder. He wanted to be back in
the safety of the orphanage as quickly as possible and this
day had already been more than strange enough for him.

Still, the further he went, the more he wondered if he
shouldn't go back without the groceries and wait until morning. He knew the way to town; he'd been there and back a
hundred times on errands, and this wasn't the right way.

Nor was it the left way.

Christopher had no idea where he was.

He didn't know how it was possible. He was certain
that there was only one road from Woodrow Children's Asylum to the town. Snake-like though it was, there were no off-
road turns to make. The forest around the asylum was too
thick for him to have gone off the road without noticing, but
he had no other explanation.

The headlights illuminated something nailed to a
tree and Christopher tottered the car toward it. There was a
sign posted on it that read: 'Keep Out: No Trespassing'

Christopher looked to see if there was an alternate
road to take, but there wasn't, and he was *quite* certain that
there were no private roads on the way to Woodrow. He really must have gotten mixed up somehow... but if there was a
private road, then there must be a residence nearby where
he could stop and ask for directions.

The rain was coming down harder, and the weak
windshield wipers couldn't keep the view clear. He pressed
on slowly, resisting the urge to put the car in reverse. The
children needed food and medicine and Mickey hadn't eaten
yet. Christopher had a job to do, a duty. Besides, if he came
back empty-handed, Madam Margot was likely to lock him
out and make him suffer through the cold night without so
much as a blanket.

'This Way'

'That Way'

'No Way'

'Yes Way'

It must have been the work of some teenagers from the town having a bit of fun, posting nonsensical signs in the woods to confuse people who were probably lost already if they were that far out in the forest.

'Up'

'Left'   'Right'

'Down'

Christopher sighed and turned right. Surely if he kept going, no matter how lost he was, he would reach civilization eventually and be able to buy groceries and get a map. At the very least, he'd be able to get directions back to Woodrow and make his way to the asylum from there.

'Watch Out'

This confused Christopher more than any of the other signs, because there was nothing in this part of the road to watch out for. The road widened, and Christopher recognized the old, bent oak whose branches stretched over his head. Relief washed over him as tangibly as the rain had. This was the right way after all! It only looked strange because of the storm.

Christopher pressed the gas pedal harder in his eagerness to finish the errand and return to Woodrow. His heart ached when he thought of the children, alone and scared on a dreadful night such as this, but it ached more to think of them without much-needed medicine.

The earlier conversation with Mickey replayed in his mind. He had left the asylum after all.

But I'll come back, he thought. *I'll always come back for the children.*

The rain continued to pour down faster than the creaky windshield wipers could deflect it. Christopher squinted at the road ahead, straining to see through the drops. The car accelerated at a steady pace.

Did Mickey really think that Christopher would leave him? Christopher imagined it for just a moment—taking the car and going away somewhere far, far away, where no one knew who he was, to get a job where he could actually keep his money and use it to start a new life—and shook his head.

I'll always *come back for the children.*

Christopher tilted the wheel to round a corner without slowing down. The children were everything. At least he had a few fleeting moments of freedom on these supply runs.

The headlights illuminated a small figure standing in the road and Christopher slammed on the breaks, twisting the wheel hard to avoid hitting it. The wheels skidded on the slick pavement and the car lurched, careening toward the side of the road and colliding with the wooden rails. The rails broke and the hood of the car passed through them.

Inside, Christopher was thrown back and forth. He struck his head on the wheel, but remained conscious. Groaning, he sat up, looking back toward the road. Had he hit the child?

Through the dark and the rain, Christopher saw the figure, thin with messy hair. They locked eyes.

"Mickey...?"

The car shifted and fell over the cliff.

Nailed to the underside of one of the branches was a small sign that read:

‘Too Late’

CHAPTER TWO

Christopher landed with a harsh *THUD* that forced the air out of his lungs, leaving him wheezing for minutes before he regained his senses.

The first thing that he noticed was the lack of the car, but he couldn't dwell on it for long. He tried to sit up to look around only to find that he was strapped to a gurney. He had to make do with turning his head from side to side.

The musty hospital room looked and felt much more like a prison cell. The door was heavy steel and the barred window was boarded up from the outside. He could hear rats scurrying along the floor.

For a moment he simply lay there in a daze as his heart rate slowed and memories emerged from the hazy fog of his mind. He remembered leaving the asylum and driving to town. Had he gotten into an accident? Something like that. He remembered swerving out of the way of someone— *Mickey? No, impossible*—and then falling.

I must have fainted, he reasoned. That was why it felt like only seconds had passed since he'd been in the car. Someone must have found him unconscious in the woods and brought him to a hospital, though this wasn't any sort of medical center that he recognized. He must have gotten mixed up in the storm and driven in the complete opposite direction from Woodrow. On an impossibly similar road.

There was a loud groan from the hallway outside, not unlike that which the asylum made when the heater was turned on for the first time after a long summer.

"Hello?" he called. "Is anyone here?"

His voice echoed around the room. He began struggling against the restraints. He couldn't stand the feeling of being trapped, and something was dripping from the ceiling onto his face. Judging by the dark stain above him, the likelihood of it being water was next to zero. Even if it was water, it wasn't clean.

The worn leather latches slowly gave way to his struggling and creaked out murderous accusations as they split along their already torn seams. Christopher wrenched his hands free. He did his best to ignore the icy liquid dripping down his back as he sat up to undo the buckles around his legs.

To his surprise, his body didn't feel the least bit sore. He would have thought that the fall would have broken an arm or a leg, maybe a rib or two. Yet he felt perfectly fine, aside from a minor headache.

How long had he been out?

Now upright, Christopher had a better view of the bloody scalpels and eye hooks on the counter. Several vials of different colored substances were attached to makeshift needles and plungers, as if a madman had attempted to recreate a syringe from a hazy memory. The only actual syringe was, frighteningly, lying discarded and empty near the trash bin, which was overflowing with bloody rags.

Christopher's stomach lurched at the thought of having been injected with... what? A sedative meant to calm him and put him to sleep? If he had needed to be strapped down, that was a perfectly logical answer, but every other piece of evidence told him that there was no one in the hospital who was opposed to letting him suffer. If he could trust what he was seeing at all.

He shook his head. His aversion to needles was making him paranoid, and paranoia wouldn't help him figure out where he was. There must be medical records lying around that would display the date and time of his arrival, and which would list any medication he'd been given.

He stood, which sent the rats fleeing back into their holes, and examined the countertop. There were no notes, nothing indicating when a doctor or nurse would be back to check on him. Nor was there anything to lead him to the conclusion that anyone had been there recently, or would be coming back any time soon.

Trying to simply open the door did no good. It was locked from the outside. Christopher grabbed a scalpel from the counter and tried to pick the lock, but he admittedly didn't know much about picking locks and the scalpel was too thick to be of any use.

The orderly knocked on the door.

"Hey! Is anyone out there? I'm locked in! Please help me!"

Nobody answered him. The gentle knocking turned to pounding that left Christopher's fingers throbbing, but no matter how loudly he yelled or how forcefully he struck the door, there was no reply.

He leaned against the cold metal, letting himself slide down until he was on his knees.

"Please, help me..."

A rat screeched frantically and darted out of its hole, followed by the flash of a large white paw and a set of claws. The claws raked the rat's back and caught in its haunches, ripping half of its body away as the rat continued forward. The poor creature limped a few more steps on its remaining front limbs before it died, screaming in agony and fear all the while. Christopher barely had to shuffle away from the hole before the deed was done.

The paw retracted into the hole and was replaced by the narrow face of a cat. With a horrible popping sound, another paw followed—enabled by the shoulder being dislocated—and the cat dragged the rest of its emaciated body through the hole before its shoulder clicked back into place, accompanied by grotesque crunching noises that made Christopher wince and cover his mouth to stop himself from gagging.

To say that it was an ugly cat would be an understatement. Its fur was ragged, mangy, and missing in places. Every so often an engorged flea jumped from it. It only had one eye; the other socket was a slimy, pus-filled mess. Its jaw was unhinged so that it seemed to be grinning with sharp, cracked teeth, and its tongue lolled out of its mouth through a gap where the teeth were missing, drooling endlessly at its paws. Every breath shuddered along its visible spine and ribs. The smell rising from its decaying skin soured the room.

Christopher tried not to look at it too much. At least he wasn't alone, if the cat was really there. It was hard to imagine that any animal could survive in such a sorry condition, much less remain an effective hunter. And there was a chance, after all—a chance that he clung to like a child to its mother—that he was hallucinating the whole thing thanks to the empty syringe. Soon, he hoped, he would return to reality and find himself in a perfectly normal hospital once the drug wore off.

If not, he prayed he would wake from the nightmare to Madam Margot scolding him for oversleeping.

The cat began to eat its monstrous meal. Minding its brittle teeth, it started where the rat was split in half, stripping scraps of meat away from the scraggly, wiry fur and tough skin. The cat worked its way up to the soft tissues and organs that were encased by bone, crushing them in its grin as they popped and crunched.

When it was done, it did not bother to clean the blood from its crooked mouth or its paws. Instead, it receded backwards into the rat hole, until Christopher could only see its smiling maw. Then it was gone. He was again alone with the stench of blood and death and fear, still leaning on the door that would not open, scalpel in hand.

Christopher didn't know how long he sat there.

When he dared to look again at the rat carcass, he saw it was quivering. Swarms of ants were moving on and through it, picking up miniscule scraps of flesh that were too small for human eyes to see. It wouldn't be long before the rat was decomposed entirely, and Christopher would still be there with the scalpel.

The scalpel.

Its tip had been stained so deeply from old blood and rust that it was almost black. Though Christopher was not fond of the idea, not just yet, it did provide a way out of the room. Then the cat would pick around the skin of his wrists and arms, sinking its teeth into his muscles and empty veins. It would move from his arms to his neck to his chest, gnawing through his organs and entrails, all the way down his legs and to his feet. Its insatiable hunger would not permit it to stop until every edible morsel had been claimed from his corpse.

The ants would take whatever was left, right down to the bone, harvesting his marrow...

Christopher shuddered but did not throw the scalpel aside.

He instead tried singing a song, but his shaking, quavering voice only made his fear audible and therefore more real. He was not yet willing to give up the idea that all of this *wasn't* real, so he stopped halfway through the second verse of "London Bridge is Falling Down." The lyrics hadn't sounded like they were coming out right, anyway.

The rat was nothing but a pile of bones when Christopher peeked again.

How long had he been there? Minutes, hours? All time seemed to blur together. He tried counting to sixty in his head, but he kept counting faster or slower, and it was impossible to be sure if he was being at all accurate. Not that it mattered; he didn't know how long he'd been there in the first place, so knowing how long *after* that wouldn't give him a good estimate of the duration of his imprisonment, even if he could calm himself long enough to sort it out.

He stared at the bones. What had been a living animal in front of his eyes not long ago (or so he thought) was now nothing. Just a pile of polished white souvenirs, a morbid monument to a life that was no more.

Was that what he would be? Had he really struggled all his life, worked himself to exhaustion every day at the asylum, just so he could end up as a pile of bones in a forgotten hospital room?

Christopher almost wished the cat would come back. Grotesque thing that it was, at least it was alive, if only just barely. It had the will to survive that he was starting to lose.

He couldn't think such depressing thoughts. He had to find a way to distract himself.

"Once upon a time... once upon a time..."

Even though he had read fairy tales to the children often, occasionally more than three times a day when they were particularly upset or wound up, he couldn't recall any to tell himself.

Instead, he found himself imagining what the source of the bloodstains on the ceiling could be and watching the drip of the red liquid onto the gurney. He tried to time the rhythmic fall to seconds, but sometimes the drip was faster and sometimes it was slower. He tried to pretend that the stain overhead was just some kind of mold, but the strong smell of iron was more convincing than his own mind. Christopher had never been much good at playing pretend.

Worst of all, he felt as if someone was watching him. Every so often, out of the corner of his eye, he thought he saw someone standing at the door or peering in at him through a crack in the boards that blocked the window. As soon as he turned and fixed his gaze fully on the shape, it vanished, probably never there at all. Just the light playing tricks.

Still, the orderly curled himself inwardly, bringing his knees to his chest and squeezing them between his arms. It made him feel less exposed, despite the lingering sensation of being spied on.

Christopher closed his eyes. Maybe if he could go to sleep, he would wake up back in his room at Woodrow, and it would be the start of a bright new day. Or perhaps he would wake to doctors and nurses explaining what had happened to him. He couldn't feel any injuries; his head ached and his stomach was turning from nerves, but there were no broken bones or bruises as far as he could tell. Maybe he had slept through his entire recovery, in which case he might wake up to Madam Margot driving him home to Woodrow. He would be so relieved to be back with the children, and he was certain that they would be happy to see him, too. Change was not something that most of them adapted to well, even when it was positive; a negative change like losing their caretaker without warning was more than likely to shake them up.

He tried to imagine the homecoming. He didn't fool himself into believing all the children would have missed him; there were a few that would have been indifferent to his absence, if they noticed at all. Most of them, though, would be delighted to have him back. They would want to talk and play and hear all about where he'd gone to for so long, and why he had left them alone with no one to care for them, didn't he know they needed him, they didn't have any food or medicine and it was *his fault* for failing to retrieve the supplies—

Christopher opened his eyes with a start. They rested on the scalpel.

The scalpel. It glinted invitingly, amiably. Hungrily.

Temptation throbbed through the young man's fearful heart.

Death was so imminent.

So imminent.

Wouldn't it be better to die on his own terms than to starve? He was sure the rat would have preferred a clean kill over being ripped in half.

It wouldn't hurt for long. He'd probably fall unconscious and slip quietly away.

Christopher began to press the dull blade to his wrist and tried to ignore the discoloration and gross buildup on the instrument. He was going to die, after all, wasn't he? It was no time to be concerned about hygiene.

A sudden noise, enhanced a thousand times and made alien by the preexisting silence, made Christopher jump. The scalpel flew out of his hand and skittered to a stop in a dark corner on the other side of the room.

Moments after the initial shock, he recognized the sound as footsteps.

Christopher wasted no time in pounding on the door with renewed vigor, his previous despair forgotten entirely.

"Hey! Hey, over here! Please, if you can hear me, help me! I'm locked in, I don't know how I got here, I'm scared—please help me!"

Much to his delight, the steps grew louder and louder. Soon they were near the door. He let out a sigh of relief when he heard the footsteps stop on the other side of it, going as far as to weep in joy. This time there definitely was a figure standing outside.

Finally, he would have answers, an explanation, a way home, a way out, salvation. He wasn't going to die after all, and he laughed at himself for being so overdramatic. Surely the doctor had just been busy with his other patients. Yes, that was probably it. Or maybe Christopher had woken up a little bit earlier than expected, and he hadn't been waiting nearly as long as he'd thought. Why, it had probably only been a half an hour, or maybe an hour at the most! Soon he'd be back at Woodr—

The footsteps continued down the hall.

When Christopher tried the door, he found it was still locked.

"What?" he gasped.

Gradually the footsteps became quieter, pausing occasionally, but always diminishing, becoming fainter, until they stopped being audible altogether.

"No! No! Come back, come back! Please! Anybody! Please... help me..."

Christopher fell back to the floor—not in a slow slide like before, but all at once, sobbing into his hands.

Why? Why was this happening to him? What had he done to deserve this?

It's because you didn't do your job right, he told himself. *You got lost and didn't get the food and medicine in time and now you're going to die in this horrible hospital room. You let every single one of those children down.* Deep in his mind he knew it wasn't true. His job at the asylum had nothing to do with his current predicament, but he had to blame *something*... and the only thing he had to blame was himself.

And now the scalpel was gone, and he didn't have the heart to stand and retrieve it.

"Don't cry, Christopher Robinson."

Christopher raised his head from his hands to see Mickey sitting on top of the gurney.

"Mickey? What are you doing here? How did you get— "

"None of that matters." The boy hopped off the gurney and knelt beside his caretaker. "Don't cry. It never helps anything."

"Are you really here?" Christopher asked, hoping against hope that he was beginning to return to reality. Maybe he had succumbed to some strange mold in the West Wing's hallway and that was why things had gotten strange after he'd left it; perhaps the hospital room was just a hallucinated version of Mickey's bedroom and he'd never left at all, or he'd fallen asleep there and everything after had just been a horribly realistic nightmare. He would have to be more careful in the future.

"Yes, I'm really here, never mind how. You will understand later."

The room remained as it was. If Christopher was coming back to reality, he was doing so at a snail's pace. Still, Mickey's familiar face made everything more bearable. He found the strength to rise and embrace the child, somehow managing to smile.

"You don't know how happy I am to see you," Christopher said. "I've been having the most awful nightmare you could imagine and I can't wait to be home!"

"It isn't over yet. You still have such a long way to go, Christopher," Mickey answered, his voice barely above a whisper.

"What do you mean?"

Mickey didn't answer his question. Not surprising, given that Christopher had noticed he wasn't in much of a question-answering mood lately. Instead, the child said, "Do you remember what I told you in the asylum? That you have to listen to what I say?"

"I remember."

"Will you? Will you do what I tell you to do?" Before Christopher could respond, Mickey continued: "I won't ask you to do anything too difficult. Nothing outside of your ability. I just need you to do what I say. Can you do that for me?"

His tone disturbed Christopher. Why would Mickey ask him to do anything in this strange place? What did he know that would allow him to give Christopher orders?

And yet, he felt strangely compelled to acquiesce, if only to appease the child. "Okay. I'll listen to you."

"Good. I've opened the door. Come find me as quickly as you can."

Christopher opened his mouth to ask what Mickey meant, though he wasn't sure what good it would do, but he found that Mickey had disappeared and he was hugging air.

His shoulders sank. Alone again. He had only imagined the encounter.

He tested the doorknob, just to see if his newest hallucination had spoken the truth. It turned in his hand—but he was sure it had been locked just moments (or perhaps hours?) before, and there was no way that Mickey, or rather the *image* of Mickey, would have been able to unlock it from inside the room.

Christopher shook his head. Stranger things had happened already. He retrieved the scalpel and escaped through the door.

The hallway beyond the room looked like it belonged in a high security prison rather than a hospital. All the doors were windowless and made of steel, and Christopher couldn't hear any noise, man-made or otherwise, coming from behind any of them. Despite the fact that the hallway ended not far behind him, and he hadn't heard the footsteps come back or any doors open, it was completely deserted.

Christopher knocked on the door across the hall experimentally. There was no noise from the other side. He moved left and knocked on the next door, too. Silence again. The same result came from the last door on that side of the hall.

Discouraged but not yet willing to give up, he decided to test the doors on the same side as his room. From the first on that side came the sound of soft weeping, which persisted no matter how much he tried to comfort the room's occupant. Getting answers as to where the hospital was and what the doctors were doing was out of the question.

When he knocked on the next door he was instantly met with vicious snarling. The door shook as whatever was on the other side slammed against it again and again. Christopher sprang backwards with a hand over his heart as the room's vicious inhabitant raged for several more minutes, until blood pooled from beneath the door and silence fell once more.

There was only one door left at that end of the hall-way, and all Christopher could hope for was that something nasty didn't answer his final knock.

"Hello?" a quiet voice called when he rapped on the door.

The young man's heart soared. Finally, another human being had responded to him! His prayers were answered!

"Hello! Can you get out of the room?"

"No, the door's locked."

"I'll see if I can get it open from this side. Hang on just a moment!"

"Cracker?"

"I'm sorry, I don't have any food with me. Ah, the door's locked on this end, too. I'll see if I can..." Christopher aligned the point of the scalpel with the lock and jiggled it from side to side to see if he could force it open. It hadn't worked with his door, but who knew? Maybe he'd just been too nervous to get it to work right.

"Hello?" the voice repeated.

"I'm still here. It's just taking a little longer than I thought."

"No, the door's locked."

"I know, I'm working on it."

"Cracker?"

"Umm..."

Christopher pulled the scalpel tip out of the lock and set it aside. Maybe there was a hairpin or, more likely, a rusty nail somewhere that might do the job better. If he was really lucky, which he was doubting at this point, he might even find the key.

The unexpected click of the lock releasing its hold echoed through the hallway. Christopher paused, frowning at the door.

"Cracker?"

Christopher turned the knob and it yielded easily. Maybe he had managed to trick it loose with the scalpel after all, though it certainly hadn't felt that way to him.

Blood stains and feathers covered the floor of the room inside. On the walls were paintings of blurred, frantic shapes, like a startled flock of birds taking wing. Fading afternoon light filtered in from the blind-covered windows and gave the crimson floor stains the appearance of fire. The room had no furniture behind which an occupant could potentially hide, and—more surprisingly—no occupant.

Christopher didn't want to think about that, and instead headed to the window to search outside. If he could spot a street sign from his vantage point, he might be able to figure out where he was in relation to Woodrow. He'd studied maps of the surrounding area plenty of times and a hospital was sure to be on a main road.

Looking down, he saw that he was on what appeared to be the third floor of the building. Dead, gray trees groaned in a hot, sweeping breeze that made tornadoes of dust, their branches scratching spitefully against the walls.

Beyond that was nothing.

There was no sky, no sun, no horizon. The world just stopped, save for the mangy cat that was stepping into the nothingness on the ground below. As it walked, it slowly succumbed to the emptiness, breaking apart and fading away until it, too, was nothing.

Christopher backed shakily away from the window, out of the room, and into the hallway where he retrieved the scalpel and held it close to his heart for protection.

His heart almost stopped when he saw shadowy figures standing behind each of the now un-boarded windows. They were too blurry for him to see their eyes, but he didn't need to see them clearly to know they were all staring at him. He could feel a hard gaze boring into the back of his head from the empty room he had just fled, and when he turned he saw a silhouette behind the window of that previously empty chamber, too.

For a long moment, Christopher stood as still as a statue, hardly daring to breathe.

Look away! Stop staring at me, he wanted to yell, but he knew he couldn't. He didn't dream of asking the apparitions for help.

His socks felt wet. He glanced down and discovered the blood that had been pooling outside of the door of the unknown, vicious creature was now starting to run down the hall. It puddled around his feet and seeped right through his old, hole-riddled shoes. He curled his toes in disgust, only to hear the faint squish of his blood-dampened socks pressing against themselves.

When he looked up again, the shadowy apparitions were standing outside the doors. They were featureless, just black shapes standing in the hall, all of their blank faces turned on him.

Christopher almost dropped the scalpel in shock. He hadn't heard any of the doors open or close, no footsteps or turning knobs, nothing. The figures were simply there, behind the doors one minute and in front of them the next.

And there had been one such shade in the room behind him, too.

He felt frigid breath on the nape of his neck.

He ran down the hall as fast as his legs would carry him. Mad cries and shouts followed close on his heels. The snarling of a giant, yet unseen beast dogged his footsteps. He was nearly at the hallway's end when the doors began banging open, some of them flying right off their hinges and into the opposite wall mere seconds after he passed them.

Behind each doorframe was now a wide, staring, bloodshot eye, twitching and moving to follow Christopher as the not-quite human things pursued him.

The end of the hallway came closer and closer with every step. The orderly wouldn't let himself think of what might lie beyond this terrible place, or that whatever came next might be worse. He needed to get down to the first floor, out of the hospital, and he'd figure out everything else from there. He just had to survive that long. He could do it.

He focused all his energy on running, and on his brief encounter with Mickey. Cryptic as he was, the child *had* told Christopher to come find him, which meant he was somewhere to be found. The thought of seeing his favorite charge again, of going home safely together, kept Christopher sprinting to the unopened door at the end of the hall. If there was a way out, it was behind that door.

A cold, clammy hand wrapped around his ankle, causing him to pitch forward and fall into his own waiting shadow. The rest of the shadows had caught up. They grabbed at every inch of him; fat fingers and slender claws ran through his hair, across his body, over his mouth and nose to suffocate him. They crawled over him, entombing him as their ethereal bodies became sticky like tar and mortar to bury him alive. Some of the inky darkness got into his mouth and he retched against its bitter taste, but it stuck fast in his throat, as if he wasn't having enough problems trying to breathe already.

He tried to push the shadows off, but it was impossible. There was nothing to fight back against but pressure, like he was struggling against gravity itself. He wrenched one arm free and reached up as the darkness covered his face entirely. Now he could no longer see, nor hear, nor breathe at all.

But he could feel.

He could feel the crushing weight, the movement of the creatures, the cooler air reaching his hand and the fingers that wrapped around his own. Fingers, five of them, small; Christopher had held hands with children often enough to recognize what this was. A child had come to his rescue.

No, run! he thought, giving the hand a squeeze. *Don't you see the monsters? You're in danger! Run away and save yourself!*

Just when Christopher thought the shadows would swallow him completely, he began to feel the pressure lifting. The bodies above him burned away into ashes.

He coughed, clearing his lungs of the smoke left behind and filling them again with deep gasps of cleaner air. He focused his eyes on his outstretched hand, where he could still feel something between his fingers. Instead of a hand, however, what he found gripped tightly in his fist was a golden key. There was no one else in the hallway, which was once again completely devoid of life and sound. All the windowless doors were back on their hinges, the floor was tidy, and his socks felt as dry as ever.

Christopher examined the key. It was thick and tarnished with age, not unlike the one that Madam Margot kept with her that unlocked the great front door of the asylum. For a moment Christopher wondered if she might have been there to come and get him after all, but that was even more preposterous than being attacked by wraith-like mutants.

Christopher headed for the door that led to the stairwell, key and scalpel in hand.

CHAPTER THREE

*R*ather than going all the way down to the first floor, the stairs were impassable past the second story landing. Beyond that, they were completely blocked off by police tape and traffic cones, and Christopher didn't like the idea of trying to get over or around the obstacles. There might be an alternate way down that didn't run the possibility of falling and breaking his neck.

He ventured instead onto the second floor, which was pristine white. Fluorescent lights shone down from almost every square foot of the ceiling. The nauseating smell of cleansing chemicals stung Christopher's nostrils.

Like the floor above, the second was comprised solely of a hallway and patient rooms. There were no lobbies, no waiting areas, no receptionist desks or pharmacies, just a row of doors on either side of the solid, white tile. He hadn't yet decided whether the better lighting with which to see was a true improvement or not. Odds were good that he would soon go blind if he continued to stare at nothing but whiteness.

Christopher peered through one of the door windows to find a white bed and a white chair sitting behind a white desk with white drawers. In the middle of all this, a tuxedo kitten was washing itself. Its fur was still the spiky fluff of a newborn. The simple contrast of having something that wasn't white to look at was a relief, and Christopher grabbed the doorknob. He wanted to see if the kitten might be socialized and make a good companion for the children if he could successfully rescue it. When he tried turning the knob, he discovered the door was locked and the golden key didn't fit. He wasn't sure why he'd expected anything different.

The kitten had heard the doorknob being twisted unsuccessfully and looked at the window with one eye. The other, Christopher noticed, was closed and a little swollen, weeping greenish-yellow pus, and its jaw was hanging in a grin.

He retreated a few steps and continued down the hall. He moved from one locked door to the next, peering through windows and checking the rooms as he went in case there was someone or something useful around. Every room was empty. Not that it mattered. The key didn't fit their locks anyway, and Christopher wasn't at all surprised by that anymore. There was simply no way it could fit into one of the new, smaller locks on the modern door handles, but Christopher wasn't about to forsake it for useless. For all he knew, the key was what had driven the creatures away.

He continued down the hall and ran into a table he hadn't seen. Pain shot up his leg as he collided with the hard metal edge. It stood right in the middle of the hallway, just sitting there. On top of it sat a small container of what seemed to be multivitamins. It was hard to read the label because the writing was all in white. The only way to make the words visible was to hold the bottle up so the light reflected off of the slightly shinier type. Even then, Christopher could only make out five letters:

EAT ME

Christopher turned the bottle over and over, trying to find a list of ingredients, but he didn't see any other labeling. He set it back down; the bottle wasn't his, and he shouldn't move it. Besides, he was still under the strong suspicion that he'd already been drugged and the effects were still wearing off.

Next to the bottle, nearly invisible against the shiny, white surface of the table, were papers. The writing on them was white as well, so Christopher held one up to the light to see what it said. Luckily the letters showed up well with the light at their backs, and he was able to read all of it:

Patient No. 45; Has frequent mood swings ranging from charming and pleasant to crude and violent, usually triggered by being told 'no' or by having what he considers to be his possessions taken away from him. Was admitted to the hospital with Patient No. 46, who has proven to be far more relaxed and cooperative with doctors, puts up no fuss whatsoever. No treatment yet necessary for either patient.

Doctor's Notes: Perfect test subjects as long as they are kept together, otherwise they will struggle.

Christopher shuddered at the phrase "test subjects" and put the paper down. He picked up the next sheet more reluctantly. Whatever was going on at this hospital was anything but kind, yet it was the only possible insight he'd found that might explain his current situation.

Patient No. 317; Experiences frequent, harsh mood swings ranging from suicidal depression to murderous rage. Has been convicted of seven counts of second degree murder by reason of insanity and may be guilty of more crimes that have yet to be proven or discovered. Is undergoing anger management therapy. MUST be handled carefully. Is being treated with carbamezepine.

Doctor's Notes: Patient No. 317 is highly unstable and must only be handled by experienced doctors, and never alone. He seems to have taken a strong interest in an individual named "Christopher Robinson" that borders on obsession; he has spoken in depth about "Christopher Robinson" more than once and

"What on Earth?" Christopher gasped.

He glanced across the hallway. The room numbers were descending; three-twenty, three-nineteen, three-eighteen...

Christopher cautiously approached room three-seventeen.

There was nothing inside it.

This was not the same sort of nothing he'd witnessed in the other vacant rooms, which had been devoid of patients and anything but standard furniture. There was *nothing*. Just like when he'd looked out from the window on the third floor, his vision was met with blind emptiness.

Christopher felt his way back to the table and grabbed the final piece of paper, holding it up. At first he could hardly read it. The writing was scratchy, sloppy, and unorganized—in some places the scrawl overlapped, making the sentences entirely unreadable. So much of it was crossed out or written over or just plain illegible that the only full line Christopher could actually read was:

They said they were going to fix me. They LIED.

The rest of what he could decipher was just two words, written over and over again:

"Christopher Robinson."

His hands shook as he set the paper down. The feeling that someone was looking at him returned in full, though he couldn't see anyone, or any*thing*, in the hallway with him. He felt around the table and cautiously walked past it, toward the end of the corridor. He was almost running in his haste to get out of the hospital, even if there was nowhere else to go. He still had a whole floor yet before he escaped the building; maybe he would find someone sane there, like a doctor or a nurse, who could tell him what had happened to him or where he was—and why he'd ended up in this place.

Or he might run into a homicidal maniac like Patient No. 317.

Or more monsters.

Either way, the risk was worth not having to spend another minute in the white hallway.

His mad dash was interrupted by the quiet sobbing of a child coming from one of the rooms to his right. He slowed and approached the door, expecting something vile to jump out at him.

Instead he found the only occupied room on the floor. Inside was a young boy with messy brown hair.

"Mickey?" Christopher exclaimed, grabbing the door handle tightly and yanking. As expected, it didn't turn to let him in, the key didn't work, and he couldn't pick the lock with the scalpel. "Mickey, I found you! Mickey!"

The boy didn't seem to be able to hear him. He kept crying. Even when Christopher pounded on the door, kicking it to the point where he thought for sure either the door or his leg would break, Mickey didn't so much as look up.

Christopher was ready to throw the key, scalpel, and anything else he could find out of frustration when he noticed another person standing in his path to the far end of the hall.

"Hey!"

The young man took off at a run again, determined to reach this new person. For once, the figure looked normal, and was approaching him at a run as well. Maybe he too was lost and confused; even if neither one of them had any answers, it would be far better to search the hospital together than to wander around alone. Nothing good ever happened when a person was alone.

The other young man waved his arm when Christopher did. The two of them opened their mouths in unison and called out happily, "Thank goodness!"

Something was off. There was too much similarity between their movements, a synchronicity that couldn't be natural. The newcomer's words sounded more like echoes than someone else simply saying the same thing.

Christopher stopped, and as he did, so did the other man.

Now he was close enough to see clearly.

The figure's black hair was disheveled from some past, terrible struggle; his robin's egg blue eyes were tired, yet hopeful—though that hope quickly faded into despair. Christopher and the figure approached each other at the same pace, and Christopher reached his hand forward, matching the other's until they touched.

Instead of warm flesh, he met cold glass.

A mirror.

Christopher sighed, and so did his reflection. Why there was a mirror at the end of the hallway, he couldn't begin to guess, At this point, he suspected it was only there to make things more difficult for him.

He leaned closer and examined his double with more care. Goodness, he *did* look terrible! A haircut and exposure to sunlight were in order.

But Christopher wasn't wearing white scrubs like the reflection was, and he wasn't smiling. The reflection's smile was cruel, the likes of which Christopher had never made in his life, full of a malicious sort of delight and knowledge of things to come that would leave him broken and ruined beyond repair both physically and mentally.

The world behind the mirror began to turn red, blood flowing down the walls and from under the doors. Twitching, writhing masses of creatures dragged themselves down the hallway toward the reflected Christopher, who grinned wickedly as they approached.

The real Christopher turned to look over his shoulder; his hallway was still clear and safe.

When he looked back, his hand rested against a red door. Unlike the others in the hall, it was made of painted wood. The doorknob was gold, and beneath it was a large, antique lock.

Christopher had no doubt that his golden key would fit this lock. The question was: did he really want to go through the door? There was no uncertainty in his mind that something bad lurked on the other side of it. However, there wasn't any other way forward. The hallway ended there, and if there was an unobstructed staircase that led to the first floor, it had to be behind the red door.

He took a moment to steel his nerves, then inserted the key into the lock and turned it.

With a loud *click*, the door opened.

Inside, everything was charred black. The stench of smoke was suffocating. A lone operating table stood in the middle of the room, surrounded by all kinds of surgical equipment: scalpels, clamps, needles, thread (though the thin fibers had burned, and only a few blackened spools remained), and less orthodox tools like hacksaws, butcher knives, axes, and a no-longer-operational chainsaw. Why any doctor would possibly need a chainsaw—and what they might use it for—was not something Christopher cared to consider.

Lying innocently on the floor, off to the side and out of the way, was a used match.

The dim light hanging over the table flickered. The brief dimming caused the shadows to move in time, which made the room that much more unsettling by giving it the illusion of being occupied by living figures. And by all accounts, Christopher couldn't know for sure that the shadows *weren't* somehow alive and waiting to grab him again.

Christopher noted most of the drawers and cabinets around the room had been welded shut by the heat of the flames. Those that he could open put up a strong resistance.

Several folders were stacked in one drawer, each containing a complete account of paperwork on patients. Christopher flipped through a few. Though not burned, the heat had affected them for the worse, making them brittle and hard to read in places.

Patients No. 45 and 46... twin brothers. The purpose of this experiment will test the possibility of psychic links between twins... transfer tissue from one twin to the other... subjects are uncooperative.

Experiments will proceed as planned.

Transplant successful, but results inconclusive.

Patient No. 317... does not want to receive treatment... Still reacts violently to staff despite heavy medication... There is no known problem that a lobotomy cannot cure.

There wasn't anything useful, so Christopher set the folders back down and closed the drawer, not wanting to look at any more of that unpleasantness. The next drawer he managed to wrench open contained nothing but a few dry pens and deteriorating sticky-notes. The rest of the drawers were shut tight, so Christopher kneeled to open the cabinet beneath.

A charred corpse fell out and its head rolled into his lap. He sprang back, crashing into the operation table.

Maggots tumbled out of the empty eye sockets that were fixed on Christopher. Vermin flooded out of the desiccated body by the hundreds. Christopher jumped onto the table and brushed the bugs off his clothes, shivering in disgust. He looked away from the raw and naked form, arms wrapped around his middle as he fought to keep the contents of his stomach where they were.

When at last Christopher's insides had finally settled and his nerves returned to a state of semi-calm, he opened his eyes and noticed a paper clutched in the skeletal body's hand. Taking care not to step on any more bugs than absolutely necessary, he leaned down and tugged the note from the corpse's grasp. It tore a bit, but the words remained legible:

The Dream Man is coming.

Christopher didn't immediately understand the importance of the message, and he would have set it aside if he hadn't noticed what it was written on: a map. The ink was faded and hard to read, but he could make out the location of the hospital on the map, as well as other buildings nearby. It was by far the most useful thing he'd found, despite the fact that it had been handed to him by a corpse. No matter the feeling of discomfort that gave him, he couldn't throw out his only clue. He folded the map and slid it into his pocket.

"Ehm... thank you."

More and more bugs were pouring out of the cabinet. Christopher opened the other door, finding not another dead body, but a hole chewed through the wall from the other side by carrion-eating insects, leading into the unknown dark of a twisting tunnel.

Again he shuddered. The only way out was through that hole. Even if he left the room, he'd only end up back in the white hall—and if he decided to go any further back, he would return to the hellish third floor. There were no other stairs leading to the first floor... or if there were, they'd been hidden beyond his sleuthing abilities. His nerves were far too strained to go back and keep looking.

He had to go through.

Slowly, cringing at every movement, Christopher lowered himself until he was halfway into the cabinet and crawled forward.

Everywhere he placed his hands, his fingers met squirming, slick, slimy things.

Whenever he set his knees down, popping noises rang in his ears.

His arms and legs tickled, alive with dozens of small, moving creatures.

Some vermin crawling across the wood above him fell onto his back and caught in his hair.

When one dropped onto his neck and oozed into his shirt, he lurched forward and moved as fast as he could through the darkness, whimpering for the want of light, of safety, and of an environment that didn't move all around him.

Sharp pinpricks of pain peppered his flesh as the bugs bit, but he didn't care and didn't dare give thought to whether or not they were poisonous. He just wanted *out*.

He couldn't tell how far he had gone or even what direction he was moving in. He didn't feel like the tunnel had sloped downward, and the thought crossed his mind that he might be crawling through an air vent between the second and first floors, unable to find a grate that would let him out due to all the *godforsaken bugs* in this tunnel.

Christopher's arms and legs began to tremble from fatigue. How long had it been since he'd last eaten or had something to drink? He hadn't been set up on any kind of intravenous system to keep his body nourished while he was unconscious—not that the idea of *anything* from this hospital being put into his veins made him the least bit pleased. He didn't feel hungry or thirsty, but his body needed proper sustenance to keep moving. If he didn't escape the tunnel soon, he was going to drop dead in it. Then he would provide sustenance for the hundreds of horrid crawlers.

Assuming they weren't already eating him.

He fought his gag reflex at the thought. Whatever there was in his stomach, he needed to hang onto it.

Christopher shook his head in an attempt to fling some of the bugs out of his hair, but to no avail; the ones that did fall off were replaced by others. But it did help bring him out of his panic and clear his vision. He could finally see a faint light, dim in the distance but brilliant in comparison to the dark.

It was tiny, far, but he was going to reach it. He hobbled forward with renewed vigor and continued to shake off whatever bugs he could.

The light was growing brighter, closer!

It was within his grasp!

He reached for it.

His hand pushed aside gravel and rock and dirt, and he could feel grass and smell fresh, damp air.

He used both hands to widen the hole, showering himself in dirt, until he could pull himself out of the tunnel.

The passage had taken him not only out of the second floor, but out of the hospital altogether and into the cemetery next door. Behind him was a headstone that read:

Patient No. 416, liked hiding in small places.

Christopher brushed off his clothes and hair, ridding himself of the creeps that stubbornly clung to him. He patted the headstone in appreciation.

He withdrew the map from his pocket and unfolded it. The hospital—Bethlem Royal Medical Center—was circled in red. It looked like there were other buildings within walking distance that could be useful, if there was anyone in them. Who knew how far the shadow creatures had spread? He had no way of knowing if only the hospital was tainted, or whether the whole town was a lost cause. Assuming Christopher wasn't hallucinating. If he was, he hoped the visions would stop soon.

He would keep quiet about that unless someone else brought it up. There was no use in getting sent back to the hospital for rambling about shadow monsters.

Christopher double-checked his directions on the map and struck out toward the visitor information center. At least that would tell him where he was. Then he would make his way to the fire department or the police station to seek assistance in getting back to Woodrow. Hopefully he wasn't too far away.

CHAPTER FOUR

*T*he visitor information center wasn't an actual building, just a large, covered signboard next to a public restroom and a few picnic tables. Behind the glass casing was a large map of the town and its surrounding area (on which Christopher could not find Woodrow anywhere, much less the children's asylum). In the little wooden shelves beneath the map were smaller fold-out maps, brochures, and pamphlets marking all the places of interest—most notably the amusement park, historic school, hiking trails, and fine eateries. Anything and everything that might be alluring to tourists was listed. There was also a large flyer informing residents and tourists alike that Bethlem Royal Medical Center was structurally unsafe and had been condemned, thus making it off-limits until further notice.

Unlike Christopher's map, the larger version revealed that the town—named "Wonderland" apparently—was situated on an oblong island that rested in the middle of a large lake surrounded by acres of forest and no less than four different campgrounds. The nearest town was marked on the upper left corner of the map, a tiny dot reading "Liddell Falls." A single bridge connected the island to the mainland.

Christopher had never heard of such a place before, certainly knew of no island on a lake, and had no idea how to get back to Woodrow. How long had he been unconscious before waking in the dreadful hospital room? How far from home had he been taken?

According to the brochures, the bridge opened and closed promptly at six o'clock in the morning and evening. He didn't bother to go check if it was still open; the sky was overcast but quickly getting darker. There was no doubt in his mind that if it wasn't past six o'clock already, it would be by the time he got to the bridge.

He would just have to wait until morning and get a room at a local hotel in the meantime, but first he had to get medical attention; the hospital might be closed, but last he'd checked, policemen and fire fighters received some medical training and would be able to help him find his way back home. They might even be able to tell him why he was in Wonderland. Someone had to have brought him here, and it only made sense that it would be someone from an emergency response crew. He tucked his faded map into one of the wood pockets and selected a new one that focused on the amenities of the town. There had to be someone who could help him.

Christopher traced the path from the information center to the police station on the new map. It wasn't far, but in a town so small he didn't expect it to be. He might be able to reach it before the sun set if he walked at a fast pace.

If ever anyone had walked as if their life depended on it, Christopher did that evening.

The streets were empty. Christopher was used to quiet and isolation thanks to the asylum, but that was in the middle of nowhere; of course there wouldn't be traffic or people in a forest that was at least half an hour's drive from anything. But for there to be not a single car moving at sundown in the heart of the town, small or not, seemed highly unlikely and more than a little eerie. Even if the bridge closed at six, there should still be people traveling from the amusement park at the other end of the island to their hotel rooms, returning home from the grocery store, maybe even going out to eat. It might be after the bridge's closing time, but it was not late by any means.

There were cars, but they were all parked on the sidewalks. They looked more than a little rusty. Spiderwebs far thicker than any Christopher had ever seen connected the tires to the streets and sidewalks. As if they were rooting the cars in place. Ignoring that, Christopher wondered for a moment what had become of the Volkswagen he'd crashed. It was probably damaged beyond use, but maybe someone in town would know for sure.

It wasn't just the cars that were abandoned on the side of the road. There were all manner of things lying in the street that were covered in dust and spiderwebs: loose bits of litter, flyers for events long since passed, dead Christmas trees, and things that shouldn't have been left out like basketballs, porcelain dolls in expensive dresses, and clothes in pristine condition. Things that would be missed by their owners and surely sought out before the cobwebs could gather, Christopher thought. So why had they been left to rot?

Thankfully the light at the police station was on. That welcome sight put a stop to his curiosity before it could take him somewhere he didn't want to go.

A small bell rang over the doorway as Christopher stepped inside the station. It was a perfectly normal noise, yet after the consuming silence of his lonely walk, it made Christopher nearly leap out of his skin and turn to see what had made the jarringly cheerful sound. The offending bell shivered to a stop on the bright red ribbon that was tacked to the doorframe.

"H–hello?" he called nervously. Hopefully there was someone there and this wasn't another empty, bloody room.

The station was small, of course. The room Christopher was standing in consisted of nothing more than a desk and a couple of overnight holding cells that were scarcely large enough for someone to lie down in. It was more reminiscent of an Old West prison than a proper police station, but there were no blood stains or dead bodies as far as Christopher could see. However, the cells could do with a good scrubbing and the toilets were absolutely disgusting. To his right, there was a door that had "Sheriff Godwin" engraved in a nameplate next to it.

The door was locked, and there was no answer when Christopher knocked. He sighed. Was the whole town abandoned?

Who had turned on the lights, then? As dilapidated as everything else was or was steadily becoming, the lights in the station couldn't have been left on for as long as the town had been abandoned. They would have burned out after about a month of constant use.

He sat on one of the soft, cushioned chairs that lined the wall adjacent to the office door. He was tired, physically and mentally, and he needed to rest if he was going to have any chance of making it out of the town before six o'clock the next day.

He sank further into the seat as his eyelids fell heavily and refused to open again.

So tired...

It wasn't long before he drifted off into an uneasy but deep slumber.

"Help! Help me!"

Christopher opened his eyes slowly, still within the grips of drowsiness. How long had he been asleep? He felt as though he'd hardly closed his eyes, but it was much darker outside than when he had arrived at the station.

"Help!"

Fully awake now, Christopher jolted up from his seat when a blond police officer dragged a thin brunet man into the station. It was the brown-haired individual who was crying for help, and there was little wonder why: he was handcuffed and in a headlock, struggling to free himself. His face was somehow simultaneously pale and turning red as he gasped for air.

"Um... should you be doing that?" Christopher asked tentatively. He didn't want to get on the wrong side of either of the only two living people he'd yet seen, and it felt more appropriate to say something related to what was happening than gush about how relieved he was to see normal people or start right in with his problems.

The officer looked up at him, just noticing his presence. He flashed Christopher a smile that wouldn't be out of place on the prince of a fairy tale. "It's fine. We do this all the time. Don't we, Michael?"

The other man—whose name was apparently Michael—did not respond. The officer kicked open the door of one of the cells and pushed him inside, then locked it.

"Now, you stay in there tonight and quit causing trouble. You know the rules."

Michael nodded and grumbled some kind of agreement, sulking in a corner of the cell like a child who had been scolded. He didn't say or do anything else, so Christopher dismissed him as being unhelpful to the situation at hand.

The officer turned his attention back to Christopher.

"Sorry about that. Kids—what can you do?" He held out his hand. "I'm Morgan Godwin, town sheriff. Nice to meet you, Mister...?"

Christopher took the sheriff's hand and shook it, glancing back into the cell. Michael looked to be Morgan's age, if not older. Definitely not someone Christopher would have called "kid."

"I'm Christopher Robinson. It's nice to meet you too, sir."

Morgan laughed. "Sir? Do I look old enough to be called *sir*? Nah, just Morgan is fine by me. Officer or Sheriff Morgan, if you find it absolutely necessary. So what can I do for you, Chris?"

It took Christopher a moment to respond. After wandering alone for so long, he wasn't sure how to reply to a question.

"I was wondering if you'd heard of a place called Woodrow. It's sort of out-of-the-way from any big cities, but it's my home, and I need to return as soon as possible. I honestly don't know when or how I arrived here, either. I'd be grateful if you could tell me anything."

Morgan frowned. "Sorry, I can't help you there, as much as I'd like to. Even if I knew where this Woodrow place was, the bridge is out. There's only the one that leads off of the island, so everyone is pretty much stuck here for the time being. As for how you got here..." He shrugged, "You look *vaguely* familiar, but I definitely don't remember bringing you here, and I'm the only kind of emergency response personnel this island has."

"But I must have gotten here *some*how. Are there any boats? A ferry?"

"Nope."

"When will the bridge be fixed?"

"I don't know. I suggest you make yourself comfortable in the meantime. There's a couch in my office that you can sleep on for as long as you need to."

"Shouldn't I go to a hotel?"

"Maybe later, but you don't want to be out there at night. Trust me." Morgan took a ring of keys off his belt and locked the front door, then closed all the blinds. The sheriff gave Christopher a more thorough once-over while he unlocked his office door. "Uh, there's some spare clothing in there, and a bathroom. You might want to use them."

Christopher glanced down and realized how filthy he was. Crawling through bugs and dirt and God-only-knows what else had taken its toll on him. His clothes sported a new layer of mud-brown coloring, and all kinds of muck and grime had gotten under his fingernails and in his hair. He could still imagine the feeling of things crawling around underneath his clothes. The sensation sent chills of disgust running up and down his spine.

"Oh, right."

He grasped the doorknob in his grimy hand, turned it, and stepped into the office. It was remarkable how much relief an unlocked door could bring after his episode at the hospital.

Morgan's office looked more like how Christopher imagined a college dorm room, sans textbooks. The desk was covered in napkins and wrappers from a place called "Godwin's Deli," with things scribbled on them like "Marinara Meatball Marvel" and "Turkey-Ham Combo Supreme." Wrinkled uniforms littered the floor and fold-out couch, mixed in with rumpled bed sheets and blankets. The adjacent bathroom squeezed a sink, toilet, and shower into its confines, none of which looked like they had been thoroughly cleaned in years.

Christopher turned on the sink and washed his face and hands, scraping out dirt from underneath his fingernails first. He could hardly hope to wash the rest of his body if his hands were so dirty that they smeared the mud around.

When he was halfway clean again he peeled off his clothes and washed the remaining scum off himself in the shower. The hot water seemed to melt the dirt and bug guts away, and with them went the horrific memories of the ordeal, gradually fading until they felt no more real than a nightmare. Never had Christopher been more appreciative of indoor plumbing, and he stayed in for several minutes longer than he needed. His lips actually curved upward in a smile, a feeling that had almost become foreign. When he finally got out of the gentle spray he changed into a spare pair of pants and a shirt that were hanging on the back of the bathroom door. They were a little big on him, but not to the point of falling off.

He decided he would burn his own clothes later. Or maybe he would throw them into the lake. They certainly wouldn't be wearable ever again.

Christopher stepped out of the bathroom and found that Morgan had made an attempt at cleaning the office. The clothes that had been tossed around haphazardly had been picked up and folded—albeit somewhat sloppily—on the desk, which had also been cleared of its wrappers. A wastebasket that had not been visible before was full to the brim.

"Sorry for the mess. I don't get much time to tidy up, and I didn't manage to get to the Laundromat this week. Anyway, you hungry? I've got half a cucumber sandwich here. I hate cucumber but when someone offers you free food, you just have to take it, right?"

"I guess so, and it's a tempting offer, but I don't have much of an appetite right now. Thank you, anyway."

Morgan shrugged and slid the sandwich off the desk, into the trash bin. The weight of it crushed several wrappers, causing them to emit an unpleasant crunching sound that nearly drowned out the clinking of glass bottles striking each other.

"Go ahead and get some rest. I'll be outside if you need me. I'd be willing to bet you have some more questions, but we'll get to that later," the sheriff said.

"Thank you. I really mean it."

"No sweat. If you need anything, I'm right outside." He grinned and gave Christopher a wink. "Unless you'd rather I stay inside?"

Christopher almost asked Morgan to wait with him until he fell asleep. He was afraid he would wake up somewhere new and terrible if another human being didn't anchor him in place. And Morgan reminded him of the kind of men he'd seen on magazine covers in the general store, strong, handsome, and effortlessly charming. If Christopher wasn't so exhausted, his heart would probably skip a beat at Morgan's smile.

He rid himself of his desperation with a shiver. He couldn't trust Morgan yet.

"No, thank you. Good night," Christopher answered as he lay down on the pull-out couch. Morgan went back to the front of the station with only a soft nod.

The sheets weren't clean and the mattress was hard, but Christopher didn't care. He was safe. There was a place where he could get food, whenever his appetite returned, and a place to sleep while he figured out how to get back to Woodrow without crossing the bridge.

All of that could wait for a few hours. He closed his eyes and was out like a light once more.

The room was small and cramped, but the breeze blowing in through the window made it feel so much more spacious.

Christopher stretched and stood, yawning on his way to the kitchen as the children began to stir. He grabbed a box of pancake mix and heated up the griddle. Even if there would only be enough for one pancake per child, pancakes were still a welcome treat at the asylum, usually reserved for "birthdays" and Christmas.

One of his favorite parts about his job was when a new child would come into the orphanage. Despite the awful implications that the child had been abandoned in the wilderness, it meant he would get to come up with another birthday to celebrate, if the child didn't know theirs. Sometimes he even got to come up with names.

When all the pancakes were cooked through, he turned off the griddle and carried one to every room, smiling at the bright response from his young charges. If only he had maple syrup, their smiles would truly light up the rooms, and the whole asylum at that. Then maybe someone would notice it was there and take one of them home.

Christopher couldn't even remember the last time a child had been adopted, but it must have happened at some point. Sometimes one or two would disappear overnight. He never met the new parents and Madam Margot never told him where the children went; she insisted it wasn't any of his business and he should stick to cleaning. He always hoped the departed children would write, but they never did.

He strolled down the West Wing with the last pancake and a glass of water, opened the door to Mickey's room, and cheerfully called out, "Good morning!"

The room was not Mickey's normal room.

It was white. All white. White walls, white tile floor, white ceiling, white furniture.

A hospital room.

On the floor was Mickey's body, drenched in gore that likewise coated the tiles, almost like he was a bathtub that had overflown. There were no apparent wounds on his body, but he looked wrong. He wasn't moving.

On the wall, written in blood, were the words, "Why didn't you save me Christopher?"

The pancake fell into the pool of blood and splashed as Christopher's legs gave way beneath him. He dropped his head into his hands.

His sobs were only broken by mournful wails. It was his fault. If he had remembered to go back to the hospital after he'd found the way out, if he had just grabbed something to smash the door window with... there had been plenty of blunt objects he could have used in the stupid operating room, but he'd only been thinking of himself. Of his own salvation. And now Mickey was dead.

It was all his fault.

Cracking noises reached his ears. He parted his fingers to see Mickey crawling towards him, or trying to, anyway. His movements were jerky and slow, glassy eyes unseeing. He wasn't frightening at all, not like the other corpses Christopher had been witness to of late.

It was Mickey, after all.

Instead of running or pushing the dead body away, Christopher opened his arms and pulled it closer, still sobbing.

"I'm sorry, I'm so sorry! I... I didn't think... God, I'm so sorry!"

In acceptance of his apology, Mickey's teeth began to rip into Christopher's flesh.

Christopher opened his eyes. He lay still for a moment, disoriented, until his mind caught up to him and he remembered where he was.

It was morning. Morgan was up and dressed in a slightly less-than-fresh uniform with a bag of dirty clothes in one hand and a bag of trash in the other. The room looked even cleaner than it had the night before, just one good vacuuming away from being halfway decent.

"Oh, hey, I was wondering when you were going to wake up. I'm heading out for breakfast. You want anything?"

"Uh, no, that's okay. I don't have much of an appetite this morning, either."

"You sure? Well, I can't make you eat, but make sure you get something. The sink water tastes pretty bad but it might help you feel better. You don't look so good, and you need to keep your strength up. Anyway, Michael's still locked up in the other room. I'll let him out when I get back so don't worry about it. If he says anything to you, don't take it too seriously. He's... well... I'm sure you'll see."

Should I ask about Mickey? Christopher thought. *I'm not sure where I am or what's really going on. I may well have hallucinated that he was at the hospital; he's probably waiting for me back at the asylum.*

"Okay. Thanks again," Christopher said.

"Sure. And I know you mentioned getting a hotel room last night, but I thought about it this morning and I think you'd really be better off staying here. It can't be easy being alone in a strange place. It's no trouble at all for you to stay."

Christopher nodded and eased off the couch. Morgan flashed him another dashing smile before he left, making Christopher wonder if the gleam in his smile was some sort of talent that needed to be used often in order to be maintained. He was sure his own smiles were never that dazzling.

Christopher made his way to the bathroom and, after handling other business, leaned down to drink from the faucet.

To say that the water didn't taste good was an understatement of an understatement. It was as if all the dirt and guck Christopher had washed off the night before had flowed into the water supply and come back out undiluted, or as if it came straight from the murky bottom of the lake. He could barely manage a mouthful; he spit out most of it and wiped away the rest with the back of his hand.

He stood over the sink for a moment to regain his composure as the taste of mud faded from his tongue. As he did, his mind wandered back to his dream, about what it might mean. Surely a dream like that had to mean something. It wasn't as if Christopher saw dead bodies and blood everywhere.

Usually.

Was Mickey really in that hospital? he wondered.

No. It couldn't be.

But if Mickey was indeed back at Woodrow, it was likely that no one was tending to him. If he could stay alive on the meager portions that the asylum provided, then he could probably go a day without eating and be alright. Hopefully it hadn't been longer than that. And Christopher didn't dare think about the alternative—that the Woodrow diet had left the children so weak that missing a single day's rations would starve them to death.

Christopher left the office, which locked behind him with a loud click. The young man glanced at the holding cell to see if the noise had disturbed the other guest at the police station.

Michael stirred and sat up. He blinked, bleary-eyed, until his vision focused and rested on Christopher. He smiled. "Good morning. Did Morgan leave?"

"Yes, just now."

"Darn. I wanted a sandwich. The kind with liver in it. You really should eat, Christopher Robinson. You'll be too weak if you don't."

Despite not having an appetite before, Christopher's stomach rumbled when Michael mentioned food. The other man was right; he really *should* get something to eat soon. He had no idea when he'd even eaten last. "Wait, too weak for what?"

"So, why are you here?" Michael went on in that ever-so-slight Southern lilt, completely ignoring him.

"I don't know. You didn't answer my question. And how do you know my name?"

"You need to eat to have energy. You know that, everyone does. As for your name, I heard it when you told Morgan."

Michael's smile became playful, like a child keeping a secret as part of some game only he was playing. It put Christopher on edge. The way Michael's eyes looked through him, like he could tell everything about him with one glance, how they followed him without moving... it was too strange and Christopher didn't like it. He turned his head and folded his arms over his chest, but he could still feel Michael watching him.

"What did you do to get thrown in here?" Christopher asked.

"Morgan doesn't like me," Michael answered with a shrug.

"But he likes you enough to give you a sandwich if you ask?"

"He can't let me starve. Or you, either. He'll bring you something. Just watch. The only reason he asks at all is so he'll know what kind to get, otherwise he gets something weird."

"I guess you two know each other pretty well, then."

"Of course. I know everything about everyone."

Christopher shuddered. He was starting to understand what Morgan had meant about not taking the prisoner's words to heart. But he definitely knew things, and that was what Christopher needed.

"I get the feeling that Morgan patrols pretty frequently. He's busy enough not to be able to clean regularly. So, has he seen a little boy, about this tall—" Christopher held his hand just above his waist. "—with brown hair and hazel eyes? He goes by 'Mickey.' Did Morgan say anything about seeing him to you when he was bringing you in?"

"He didn't say anything, but that doesn't mean he hasn't seen him," Michael responded, nearly giddy. "It would be rather interesting if two people appeared in our little town out of nowhere at the same time. I'm sure Morgan will bring it up if he's seen the kid when he gets back. Speaking of going places, I don't suppose you could let me out of here a little early? Not that I don't love confinement or anything, but it's a cramped and I'd like to stretch my legs. Morgan keeps a spare key on that desk over there."

"He said he'd let you out when he got back. You can wait a few more minutes, can't you?" Christopher wasn't too sure about Michael, and he didn't want to do anything to anger the man who had offered him a safe place to sleep.

"You don't trust me," Michael sighed. "Let me guess. Morgan told you I'm crazy."

"Not in so many words. And he didn't say 'crazy.' I'd peg you more as an eccentric, actually."

"Honest, aren't you?"

"I thought you knew everything about everyone," Christopher said with a hint of a snap. Then he shook his head. "Sorry. I'm not in the best of moods. I guess I am a little hungry, and it's making me irritable."

"You don't say. Well hey, at least you're not hungry *and* in a jail cell," Michael retorted. "So you don't believe I'm crazy?"

"No."

"Then let me out."

"I will, on one condition," Christopher said after giving it some consideration. "I want to know about Bethlem. What can you tell me?"

Michael's eyes widened and he retreated into the furthest corner of his cell, curling up into a little, quivering ball.

"Michael?"

The only response he got was the prisoner rocking back and forth, muttering something unintelligible.

"Michael?" Christopher sighed. He wasn't going to get any sort of response now. Michael's reaction only increased Christopher's desire for information about the hospital. Something awful had happened there, and whatever it was, he had a feeling it was his way out. He hadn't woken up there for no reason; no sane person would have taken him there, injured or not, and he didn't dare ask the question of how he had been found in the first place if the island's sole bridge was out. Perhaps he had been dreaming all along, and might still be dreaming. Regardless, he needed answers.

Christopher pulled the map out of his pocket and located Godwin's Deli. It was only two blocks away. He left the station and started walking.

The fog was so thick that Christopher could barely see the map in front of his face. It made sense, of course, that a town in the middle of a lake would have heavy fog in the morning and well into the day before it burned off in the afternoon. However, this fog seemed to be something more, a deliberate obstacle to prevent Christopher from reaching his destination.

What nonsense. It's only fog, he thought.

He walked slowly, checking the map frequently to make sure he was on the right path. He had to make a left turn, and he didn't want to miss the street because he couldn't see the sign.

Through the fog came a soft, skittering noise.

He paused for a moment to listen. It was so hard to place what the noise might be that at first he thought he'd imagined it, or misheard.

Behind him, the sound came again.

He turned to look but could only see fog.

The shuffling came a third time from a different direction, but hadn't come any closer as far as Christopher could tell.

He kept walking at a faster pace. He didn't want to know what was making that noise; even if he had been remotely curious, the last way he would want to find out would be by meeting it. He was almost running, searching through the fog for the street sign he knew should be coming up soon.

There! Mock Turtle Drive.

Christopher made the turn and ended up right in front of the deli.

Godwin's Deli was, of course, fairly insignificant in size. The name was hand-painted over green–and–white striped awnings that hung above the windows on either side of the door. A row of planter boxes sat on the window sills, filled with dead, brown plants that would have given some semblance of life to the place if they'd been colorful. A blackboard sat out front with the day's specials written on it:

*Breakfast Special: Peppered Pig (Bacon, peppers, and Swiss
cheese served on a toasted roll)
Lunch Special: Butter Watch Out (Chicken salad and lettuce on
a buttered croissant)
Specials served with a cup of the daily soup and crackers
Daily Soup: Oyster Chowder*

Christopher went inside to see if Morgan was still there and was greeted by the ringing of a little bell that hung over the door. It was a friendly sound; perhaps all the buildings on the main street were equipped with one.

"Hi, welcome to Godwin's Deli, home of the best sandwiches in town since nineteen-forty-six!"

"Hell—Oh, it's you, Officer Morgan. I was just looking for you!" Christopher was much better prepared to question him this time. Someone other than Michael had to know the hospital's history, and it made sense that Morgan would have some information on it. First things first, however. Christopher needed to know if there was even the slightest chance that Mickey was in the town, too. "I wanted to know if you had seen a young boy around?"

The man started laughing, and Christopher looked at him in bewilderment until he stopped.

"Morgan just left. I'm his brother, Matthew," he explained.

Christopher took a closer look. The man in front of him was blond and a dead-ringer for the sheriff, but the eyes that looked at him from beneath his green visor were light brown, not blue. And his smile didn't sparkle. "Oh, I'm sorry! You look so much alike—"

Matthew waved one hand dismissively. "Don't worry, I get that a lot. It's fine! We *are* identical twins, after all."

"But your eyes..."

"Pardon?"

"...Nothing. Anyway, since he was just here, did Morgan mention anything about seeing a little boy in town? He has brown hair and hazel eyes, and he's small for his age."

"He didn't mention anything to me at all, but I think *I* might have seen a boy wandering around before sunset last night. When I tried to call him inside he ran away. I don't know what happened to him after that."

"But you did see him, then?" Christopher asked hopefully.

"Yes—or, I think I did, anyway. This probably sounds strange, but people see all kinds of things around here when it starts getting dark."

"I'll trust your word. The last place I saw him was at the hospital, so I'm glad he got out of there okay."

Matthew's smile dropped. Christopher could have slapped himself for being so informal about mentioning Bethlem when it was obviously a delicate subject.

"Why would he have been anywhere near that place? Or you, for that matter?" Matthew questioned.

"I woke up there, and I saw him while I was trying to find my way out. I'm still curious about it, since I have no idea how I got there in the first place. That can't be normal."

"Nothing about that place is normal, and you're lucky to have made it out without being fitted for a coffin. The entire first floor was taken out by the fire, so the whole place is unstable and could collapse at any minute. So many people died… it was terrifying. If you're trying to find out more about it, I wouldn't advise you to do any field research, that's for sure."

"Thanks for letting me know," Christopher replied. At last he felt he was getting somewhere! He wasn't sure where, exactly, but it was a start. He wanted to head to the fire station and ask someone about the hospital fire, but Matthew still looked upset. Christopher couldn't leave him like that after making him drudge up what were obviously painful and unwanted memories.

Christopher put a hand on Matthew's shoulder. "Are you alright?"

"It's just something odd I remembered. I'm sure it's nothing."

"What is it?"

Matthew shifted uncomfortably. "My brother and I were in the hospital when the fire started. I was so scared, even with Morgan leading me out. I thought for sure we were going to die. And then I had a thought. It sort of came out of nowhere, but I remember thinking, 'I can't die here, because I'm already dead.' I know it sounds ridiculous. It was just a passing thought I had at the time. I'm sure it doesn't mean anything. Sometimes a dream is just a dream, right? Sometimes a thought is just a thought."

I can only hope so, Christopher thought with a twinge of worry.

Matthew smiled, shaking it off. "You look hungry. Can I get you something to eat? I wasn't lying when I said that we've had the best sandwiches in town since forty-six. Of course, we've got the *only* sandwiches in town! Soda too, if you want it. The water here is awful."

"Tell me about it!" Christopher held his now-growling stomach. "A sandwich sounds good, but I don't have any money."

"To tell you the truth, I sort of stopped caring about money. I just like making sandwiches for people. I mean, it's not like there's anything I can really do with money here, even if I had it. We all look out for each other, make sure everyone has enough to eat, shelter... it's kind of nice."

"I see. In that case, can I get a B.L.T.?"

"Coming right up! Anyway, do you mind telling me more about yourself while I get it ready? We don't get many visitors out here since the bridge closed down, so it's always interesting to hear news from outside. Would you like some soda with that? We have regular cola, diet, orange, lemon-lime, grape, and cherry cola."

"No soda, thanks. I don't like what caffeine does to me. You mean there aren't any radios or news stations where you can get your information from?" Christopher asked.

Matthew removed a small portion of bacon from the storage room and set it on a tray to heat in the toaster oven. The smell of maple and meat was wafting through the air before he answered. "None working. But enough about this old town! Who are you and what do you do for a living? What's your favorite color? Do you have a dog?" Matthew asked eagerly.

"My name is Christopher Robinson, and I work at a children's asylum. My favorite color is green. I don't have a dog but I did see this ca—"

There was a loud meow at his feet, which made him freeze. Matthew gave a goodhearted laugh and picked up the source of the meow, an adult tuxedo cat with an ugly-looking left eye that was swollen shut. It was crusty where the lids came together. Christopher flinched inwardly.

"This is my cat, Cheshire. Isn't he cute? I've had him since he was a kitten. I asked if you had a dog because he doesn't like the smell. He wanders around a lot, but he's really quite tame. I suppose he came back in because he smelled the bacon cooking. He's got one heck of a nose!"

"Uh... yeah," Christopher said. He reached out to pet the cat when Matthew held the creature up expectantly, even though he really didn't want to touch Cheshire. Considering that Matthew seemed to have a great deal of affection for the beast, it didn't seem right not to pet the proffered cat. Christopher could only hope Cheshire didn't like him enough to rub his face against his hand. "What happened to his eye?"

"I'm not sure. Like I said, he wanders. He tends to get into a lot of fights with rats, so I think maybe one of them scratched it and it got infected. There's no vet, so all I can do is clean it and hope it'll heal on its own. He doesn't act like he's too bothered by it, thank goodness. At least he isn't in pain. And his fur is so soft."

Matthew began petting the cat, who purred loudly. Although that should have been an endearing sound, Christopher couldn't get over the memory of the old, decrepit cat and malformed kitten at the hospital, both with the same eye problem. It was possible that Matthew's cat was simply from the same family and that the eye condition was some sort of unlucky genetic trait... but somehow Christopher didn't think so.

Matthew set the cat down and returned to the sandwich-making after washing his hands.

"So, a children's asylum. That must be interesting."

"It was. Is. It isn't the worst job in the world, and the children really like me. That's why I need to find that boy, Mickey, as soon as I possibly can and get back to the asylum. How long has the bridge been out?"

"I don't know. It has been for as long as I can re-member," Matthew said with a frown. "Morgan says that it wasn't always—that before the bridge burned down, campers and tourists used to come here all the time to buy supplies and eat at the restaurants and stuff. Lots of them came just for the amusement park. But then, well, the bridge burned down."

"And there's no other way out of town?" Christopher asked. "On an island like this, there must be boats some-where."

"No. All of the boats were either destroyed or went adrift during a storm the same night as the fire. Some people tried to swim across the lake, but the currents... you know."

The two observed a moment of silence before Mat-thew continued.

"It was about a year after the hospital, or maybe be-fore. It's hard to keep it all straight." Cheshire purred and rubbed his face against Matthew's pants—thankfully, not the side with the bad eye. "Cheshire, don't trip me! You aren't getting any bacon right now!" He gently nudged the cat aside.

"I find it hard to believe that the bridge wouldn't have been repaired if there were a lot of tourists coming here," Christopher said. "I would think the townspeople would get the bridge fixed up pretty fast in that case."

Matthew shrugged. "You would think. Anyway, if there was a way off the island, I'd have found it a long time ago. I'd do *anything* to get out of here."

The look in his eyes was oddly dark. It prompted a nervous laugh and a change of subject from Christopher. "How many other people live here?"

"Well, there's Terceira, she won the beauty pageant for the state once, years ago. And Michael—if you've met Morgan you've probably met Michael. He practically lives at the police station, he gets arrested for loitering and stuff a lot. He isn't really in trouble, it just kind of gives him a place to sleep, and to be honest I feel better at night knowing that he's locked up."

"I think I can agree with you on that," Christopher murmured.

"There's also Prima. I don't like her much either. She runs the bar and she's sort of violent, so sometimes she gets put in jail too, to sleep off the alcohol. And then there's Abel, he's a gardener. He used to be really famous for growing all kinds of rare hybrid roses, but he hasn't been able to cultivate any in a long time. Come to think of it, I haven't seen him around in a while. Who else... oh, Joseph and Mary run the grocery store up the road."

Matthew was silent for a minute. Christopher waited for him to continue, but he didn't.

"Is that really everyone? Just six people?" Christopher frowned. How many hundreds had drowned in their attempt to escape the town? Why would people have continued to attempt the water crossing if they'd known it would lead to death? Or maybe they'd died in the fire instead. Neither scenario was attractive, no matter how it was presented.

And all the survivors were adults. Christopher resisted a grimace. Children and adults might be equally selfish, but adults always tried to be sneaky about getting what they wanted, and they always wanted completely different things from him than children did.

"Almost everyone. There's a pretty lady I see around sometimes, but I can never catch her name. That's it unless you want to count Cheshire," Matthew responded. "Do you want mayonnaise?"

"Yes, please."

The cat hissed and ran into the back room as the bell signaled a new arrival. Matthew ducked his head, focusing very intently on making the sandwich. Christopher turned to see Michael standing behind him.

"Hello again Christopher!" the resident of the police station exclaimed loudly, wrapping Christopher in his arms as tightly as if they were close childhood friends who hadn't seen each other in years. Christopher wheezed and gasped for breath. He hadn't expected such a strong grip from such a lanky man. He coughed when he was released.

"Hello, Michael," Matthew said quietly. He didn't sound nervous to Christopher; more like he didn't want Michael to be there, but couldn't say so. "The usual?"

"And some soda. Cola-flavored."

"Of course."

"I assume that you two have met, then." Matthew forced a laugh. "Your B.L.T. is ready, Christopher."

"Yes, Christopher is my new friend," Michael said.

When did that happen? Christopher thought, but he didn't argue. Instead he took his B.L.T. and sat down at a booth, only for Michael to join him as Matthew started assembling his sandwich. The B.L.T. was lacking a few parts, specifically the L and the T, but Matthew was distracted making Michael's sandwich, and Christopher didn't want to offend him.

"Did you find out what you wanted to know?" Michael asked.

"I'm not sure," Christopher answered. The words tumbled out on their own, like the children's teeth at the asylum. "I know that I need to investigate the h—that place some more, though. Everything seems to be tied to it."

"Good." Michael smiled.

Christopher was really starting to not like it when he did that. The expression sent cold shivers down his spine, a feeling he had always hated. It wasn't like the twins' warm smiles or laughter. Even Cheshire was less creepy. And that knowing look. Michael knew Christopher wasn't comfortable with him, and he loved it.

Christopher chewed on his sandwich and considered his options. Someone, somewhere, knew how he'd reached the island, and everyone was keeping quiet about it for some reason. It was the only explanation, even if Christopher didn't know why they would do such a thing. Otherwise, why weren't they up in arms over the fact that there was a new person on an unreachable island, much less one who had wandered down from the abandoned hospital that—so far—everyone hated and feared? Morgan and Michael had pointed out the strangeness of Christopher's presence, but they'd hardly asked a single question about it.

"Here you go. Liver and onions on wheat, and your soda," Matthew said, setting the sandwich and glass in front of Michael and sitting down with them. "Is there anything else you wanted to know, Christopher? I'd be more than happy to help."

"Yes," Michael added eagerly, "is there anything else?"

"No," Christopher lied. There was no end to the questions he had, but he didn't want to ask them in front of Michael. He also didn't know how far Matthew's involvement in the conspiracy went, or even if he wanted to know. "I think I've got everything I need for now. Thank you very much."

"It's a nice day out. Maybe you should go look around town? There aren't all that many people, but there's plenty of interesting places," Matthew suggested. "And if you see my brother, tell him to eat his cucumber sandwiches or else he'll get fat!"

Christopher nodded. "Sure."

He concentrated on eating his sandwich, which was harder to do than one might think. Matthew fell silent, and Christopher could feel Michael's unblinking stare, his own sandwich untouched. It was deeply unsettling. Christopher had always hated to be watched while he ate. However, he couldn't think of a polite way to tell them to leave him alone, so he didn't say anything.

Once he was finished eating he thanked Matthew and left the deli. Only then did he remember the thick fog that awaited him outside, which was very strange. He was certain the street had looked much clearer from inside the sandwich shop.

He consulted the map again to try to get an idea of where to go next. If anyone was at the fire station, they would probably know the most about the fire, but Matthew had just informed him that the only people left in the town were himself, a sheriff, a sandwich-maker, an ex-beauty queen, a gardener, a bartender, the two grocers, a mystery woman, and Michael.

Christopher examined the map more closely.

In the town square were the police station, deli, fire station, and an assortment of general touristy shops: Unicorn and Lion Books, the grocery store, Dodo Antiques, and The Sleepy Dormouse Bar. Further down the road was the school, which taught kindergarten through twelfth grade to the local children, and the Grand 52 Hotel. The rest of the island was comprised of residential houses, woodland, and at the far end, the Wonderland Amusement Park. The bridge was supposed to be an extension of the main street, but even on the map there were harsh, scratchy lines about halfway across where it had apparently come undone.

"What are you looking at?"

Christopher jumped, and of course, there was Michael.

"Don't do that!" he scolded. "You nearly gave me a heart attack."

"I'm sorry," Michael said, looking genuinely downcast despite his ever-present smile.

Christopher sighed and patted his shoulder once. Michael scowled at him disapprovingly and he removed his hand. "It's alright. Just don't do it again, okay?"

"I won't. I just wanted to give you this," Michael answered, removing something from his pocket and placing it in Christopher's free hand. It was a miniature flashlight, the kind that someone might carry if they were on a camping trip and needed to use the bathroom in the middle of the night. "I took it from the police station. I thought it would help."

"Help what?" Christopher asked. "And you shouldn't steal things."

Michael shifted his weight from one foot to the other. "Michael? What aren't you telling me?"

The other man didn't answer.

Christopher tucked the flashlight into his pocket.

"Thank you all the same. I'm sure it will come in handy." That was a lie. Christopher highly doubted there was anything in the darkness of this town that he would want to see.

Michael beamed, and for once the expression didn't make Christopher nervous. "You know, if you're looking for a lost child, you might want to check with Joseph and Mary. They've always wanted a child of their own, and if they saw him they would probably invite him in."

Christopher cracked a small grin. "Thank you! Do you know where they live?"

"Sure. It's..." Michael took the map from Christopher and traced it with his finger, then stabbed down on a certain place. "Here! Three-one-seven, Carpenter Street."

"Thank you very much!" Christopher replied as he took the map back, checking to see where Carpenter Street was in relation to his current position. He would have to go toward the school and turn onto Tweedle Drive, make a left on Oyster Way, turn right onto Walrus Avenue, and then make another right shortly afterward onto Carpenter Street. It seemed simple enough. He tucked the map back into his pocket and took off at a run while Michael smiled and waved until he was no longer visible.

CHAPTER FIVE

Reaching Joseph and Mary's home took longer than Christopher had thought it would. The distance on the map was deceptively short. Either that, or the road was stretching as he walked on it.

Oyster Way was a nice enough street, or at least it would be in proper sunlight. The homes were all uniquely designed and painted, not like the cookie-cutter houses that were becoming popular. These houses had been designed to suit their owners' specific tastes and create unique living spaces that would never fit two people in the same way.

That made it all the more disturbing to know they were entirely abandoned. Each time Christopher saw a boarded-up window or took notice of the shaggy lawns and gardens he felt his blood chill in his veins. How many had died in the hospital fire or while trying to escape from the island? And there was a school on the island. How many victims had been children?

Christopher kept his pace brisk and hurried along the cracked sidewalk to Walrus Avenue. A faded purple trike sat in the middle of the street by itself, just barely visible in the fog. He wasn't sure why, but he had to stop for a few moments to stare at it before he could move on to Carpenter Street.

When he reached three-one-seven Carpenter Street, it was entirely different than anything he'd thus far seen. None of the houses had been close to identical, but they had all more or less had the same visible features: a yard, a front door, a few windows, and a slanted roof. This house was humongous compared with the rest, sacrificing what square feet would have been used for a yard to instead host a large front porch complete with a set of fancy patio furniture and a few planter boxes that held only pink, plastic flowers. It had three stories instead of one or two, and the second-floor balcony was lined with a white railing that made Christopher think of the scalloped icing on a birthday cake. The walls were painted a flashy pink.

The entire house screamed of luxury and little girls' dreams. Christopher was quick to associate it with a dollhouse that one of the girls at the orphanage had managed to find in a magazine clipping and asked for as a Christmas gift. Of course, he hadn't been able to buy it for her. He'd never had money with which to buy gifts. But he *had* made a modest replica out of an old chest that no one used, the handles of which were remarkably similar to the knocker on the door.

Christopher took the knocker in his hand and tapped it on the metal base lightly, not wanting to startle Joseph and Mary when they hadn't been expecting company.

It took all of five seconds for them to answer.

"Hello, hello!" said a cheery man, who Christopher immediately assumed was Joseph.

"You're just in time, I've finished frosting the cake!" the woman, Mary, added. She wore a huge smile that came right out of a dentist's fondest dream.

"Hello," Christopher responded after being dragged inside by the two grocers. "I'm sorry to have come without calling first, but I didn't have your number."

"That's quite alright!" Joseph laughed loudly with his booming voice. "Go ahead, have a seat at the table, bud!"

It wasn't as if Christopher had a choice; Joseph steered him to the large wood table in the dining room, pulled out a chair, and proceeded to practically force him into it. Mary disappeared into the kitchen. Her humming could still be heard, echoing through the house.

While he waited for her to return, Christopher noticed that almost everything in the house was pink. The walls, the cake platter, the napkins, even the curtains and the carpet. Everything was a rosy color, including the flowers growing in the vase, but he was too surprised to see *living* plants to focus on their color.

Mary carried a gorgeous, three-layered cake into the dining room and even twirled as she set it on the table. Christopher was willing to allow her that—the cake was wonderfully decorated, and she must have spent a lot of time working on it—but he thought it was a bit much when she started singing:

> *"Beautiful Cake, so luscious and pink,*
> *Waiting on a silver platter!*
> *Who in such pastries would not partake?*
> *Cake of the day, beautiful Cake!*
> *Cake of the day, beautiful Cake!*
> *Beautiful Cake, who cares for Danish,*
> *Pudding, or any other dish?*
> *Who would not give all to take*
> *A slice of beautiful Cake?*
> *Beautiful Cake, Beautiful Cake,*
> *Cake of the da-ay,*
> *Beautiful, beautiful CA-A-AKE!"*

Joseph applauded. "Absolutely wonderful, dear!"

Christopher didn't agree, but he thought that it would be rude not to acknowledge her effort, and gave a few half-hearted claps.

"Why thank you, my dear!" Mary served Joseph, Christopher, and herself slices of cake, but the married couple didn't eat. Instead, they dipped their forks toward the dessert, then raised the empty utensils to their mouths.

"Delicious!" Joseph decreed. "You've outdone yourself, honey."

"Why thank you, my dear," Mary repeated. "I've worked on it alllllll morning."

It wasn't polite, but Christopher stared at them. How could he help it? Their behavior was beyond odd. If they were waiting for their guest to take the first bite before they had theirs, why were they pretending to eat the cake?

Christopher got his answer when they turned their attention to him, eyes and smiles expectant. He threw together a generic bit of praise as fast as he was able.

"Yes, it's, um—" Was it just his eyes being affected by all the pink, or was his piece of cake actually made of plastic? He poked it with his fork. It was. "—lovely. Now, about why I'm here..."

"Would you like some wine to go with it?"

"Oh, no, I don't drink. I haven't any tolerance for it."

Mary ignored him and went to the kitchen. She returned with two glasses and placed one in front of Christopher, then poured the wine. He was actually surprised to see that pink liquid did come out of the bottle and fill his glass. Mary poured one for herself once his glass was full. She finished it almost at once and set to pouring herself another.

"Drink up! It's good for your health."

"Thank you?" Christopher replied, carefully moving the glass a little further away from him. Mary took it once she finished her second glass and drank it down, too. "I'm grateful for your hospitality, but I really can't stay long. I came here to ask you about a boy who might have passed by. His name is Mickey, and he's only about as tall as my head is right now. He has brown hair and hazel eyes. Have you seen him?"

"Why don't I check upstairs?" Joseph offered, rising from his seat. "Although he sounds a bit unruly to be one of ours, wandering about when he should be in school."

"It's not like Mickey to misbehave, though he has been acting strangely as of late. Why don't I come with you? It would probably help if he saw a familiar face," Christopher replied, but as he was getting out of the chair Mary put a hand on his shoulder. She was much stronger than he'd expected and was able to keep him in his seat easily—not that he would put up much of a fight.

"Oh no, you haven't finished your cake yet!"

"I'm really not that hungry, ma'am," Christopher said. "I just came from the deli, you see."

"But you must try a bite! And besides, if you get up, we'll lose your head height and then we won't be able to tell if our boy is too tall or too short to be the one you're looking for."

"I would know Mickey if he was twenty feet tall," Christopher remarked, mostly to himself. Mary didn't appear to hear much of anything he said, anyway. She was still staring intently at his fork and cake. To appease her, he lifted the fork and pretended to take a bite. He'd played pretend with the children plenty of times, after all, but he had never heard of an adult who was so adamant about the game.

Michael may be creepy, but these two are absolutely insane, he thought. *I'll grin and bear it if it means finding Mickey. I don't think I want him anywhere near these two.*

"Brown hair and brown eyes, you said?" Joseph asked as he came back to the dining room, holding a large suitcase.

"Hazel eyes. What's the suitcase for?" Christopher asked wearily.

The man opened the case to reveal dozens of porcelain dolls, all brown-haired and brown-eyed, staring up at them. For a moment, Christopher wondered how many other suitcases containing different hair and eye color combinations were upstairs and just as quickly dismissed the thought with a quiver of his shoulders.

"They're all rather young, so I don't think they'll be quite as tall as what you're looking for," Mary said.

Christopher stood before either of them could stop him. The very thought of Mickey as one of those dolls made him sick to his stomach. Though he was willing to admit that some of it was personal bias—he had always hated those kinds of dolls, the way they were constantly staring—if Joseph and Mary didn't have Mickey, a notion that was quickly becoming less and less disappointing, then he didn't want to remain in their home for a second longer.

"Yes, I see. Then I had better restart my search again. Thank you for the cake, it was... delicious."

He started for the door, but Joseph grabbed his wrist.

"But you must let us introduce them. They seem so excited to meet you."

Christopher looked back. All of the dolls' faces were turned toward his, their glass eyes wide and oddly expectant, excited even. Their painted-on mouths smiled wickedly at him.

"No, that's alright," Christopher said, pulling himself free. "I must be on my way. Perhaps another time."

Never counted as "another time," didn't it?

He quickly strode to the door, stepped out onto the street, and headed back toward Walrus Avenue. He hoped the grocers wouldn't follow, but he made sure that if they did, they wouldn't catch up, and certainly not if they were carrying their suitcases full of doll children.

He retraced his steps to get back to the town square and, once there, checked the map again. The school seemed like the best place to search next. After all, it was a natural place for children to be, even if, according to Matthew, there were no children left on the island. Mickey had always been hesitant of interacting with other children, so Christopher wondered if his idea was really a good one. But where else was he to look, until someone else said they'd seen the lost boy?

He was halfway there before he realized that the trike he had seen in the street earlier hadn't been there on his way back.

The fog had become thicker and more menacing, despite Christopher's earlier belief that it would burn off as the day wore on. It was cold, and he felt as though tiny icicles were stabbing his face, neck, and hands as he walked through it. His legs were starting to tire and his feet hurt, but he couldn't stop. He had to find Mickey before sundown; only then would he, the *ever-so-devoted* caretaker, rest.

He took the flashlight out of his pocket and turned it on. Its beam of light was thin and weak, and it didn't make things any easier to see. He turned it off and stowed it away, running his hand along the edges of the buildings that he passed to make sure he was still going the right way until there were no more buildings near the road. Then he walked straight down the middle of the street. He wasn't afraid of being hit by a car; they were all around him, rusted and rooted in place by ancient webbing, and he counted them as he passed. There weren't many, but he noticed that they all pointed behind him, toward the bridge. There was not a single one that had been headed into town.

What happened in Wonderland that made all its citizens flee at once?

Christopher lost count after a sudden noise reached his ears. It wasn't loud by any means. He only heard it at all because of the contrasting silence. It was an odd noise, a kind of shuffling, but at the same time scuttling. Like a dismembered insect dragging itself along with one or two remaining limbs. It was the same odd, yet distinct sound he'd heard in the fog before.

He ignored it and kept going. If he started thinking about what kind of creature could produce such a sound, he would surely begin to go mad, or at least be distracted from his goal.

It came again, closer this time, then again and closer still.

The third time it was so close that it made his ears buzz as if a fly had just zoomed past. He broke into a mad dash, feet pounding the pavement as he tried to steer himself along the road and not dart off into one of the side streets to find cover. It wasn't as if the thing—whatever it was—wouldn't follow him there, and he wasn't entirely sure that there weren't more of them elsewhere.

His lungs screamed for want of air. He took deep breaths to try to placate them, but he was exerting far more energy than he could possibly take in from the stifled and damp atmosphere. His ears were deafened by his mind yelling at him to move faster, move farther, get away get away *get away*, and he didn't even know if the thing was chasing him anymore or if it ever had been at all.

The panic made him trip over his own feet. He couldn't be sure if he'd run just a few yards or a few hundred, because the nothingness of the fog looked the same in every direction. The fall jerked him out of his aimless state and he rose to his knees. He brought out the flashlight and the map again, clutching both to his chest for comfort before utilizing either. He opened the map and shone the flashlight on it before briefly sweeping the surrounding area. He could see nothing in the mist. Whether this was a good thing or another source of anxiety, he didn't know.

He was slow to realize the futility of checking the map. He could be in the wooded area on his way to the amusement park or only just out of sight of the town square, and he wouldn't know the difference. He walked to the edge of the street to see if he could make out one of the buildings and use it as a reference point.

The school rose out of the fog in front of Christopher, and he stood before it in disbelief, still panting from running so far. For once, a stroke of luck. He should have expected things would go wrong at that moment.

The rusty steel gates seemed to grin down at him. They were welcoming in the way that a Venus fly trap welcomes a fly into its waiting mouth, almost begging him to come inside.

They weren't locked, in any case.

Christopher stepped into the schoolyard. Sparse, dead grass grew over the cracked sidewalk. The ivy that had grown and died over the building reminded Christopher of Woodrow Asylum.

The grass almost shrank away from his determined footsteps, as if it felt pain whenever the boots he had borrowed from Morgan's office strayed across one of the blades. Every one of his footfalls produced a definitive squishing noise that made him cringe; he didn't want to slip and fall into the mud or water or whatever else was causing that sound.

As he walked, Christopher noticed a graveyard of toys half-buried in the grass. Dirty dolls with eyes missing and heads on backwards quietly watched him, judged him. Jacks were laid out on the pathway like a spiked barricade. A pack of cards lay scattered about, and though he was sure he had managed to avoid stepping on any of them, a stray two of clubs stuck to the bottom of his shoe. He had to stop to pull it off before he could keep going. Toy cars were piled into a horrible collision with army men lying around it, missing limbs and heads and mangled into forms that would without a doubt result in the certain but agonizingly drawn out death of a real human.

Christopher approached the doors of the school while trying to think about it as little as possible. He ascended stairs that felt as though they might crumble under the weight of his adult form. Like the gate, the front doors to the school were unlocked; the simple turn of a handle and a gentle push opened them.

He progressed into an empty hall of rusted lockers beyond the doors. On the ground were long-discarded pieces of paper. It had been a long time since any child had attended this school, that was for sure.

A stray thought crossed Christopher's mind: it might be possible to locate old items that belonged to the residents of the town in their childhood. He brushed it aside. All that mattered was finding Mickey and, if he was there, getting him out of the creepy school and back to Woodrow.

The door swung shut behind him, slamming back into place. This wasn't unexpected in the least, given the usual habit of school doors to do this, but the sheer volume of the slam startled Christopher anyway. It was much, much darker in the hallway than it had been, nearly pitch black. When he looked through the windows of the front doors, the fog had dissipated, and in its place there were now heavy, dark clouds. Rain began pelting the ground below.

He felt along the wall for a light switch, hoping he didn't find anything else in the process, like a stream of blood or severed hand or any of the other things that a mind alone in the dark will create. He was fortunate in that respect; his hand met a plastic switch, but when he flipped it up, the hallway remained consumed by darkness.

Christopher pulled out the flashlight and turned it on. The light was still weak and didn't cover much ground, but he was able to see the papers and red crayons scattered about, and he could even make out some of the writing on the papers he passed. Unfortunately none of the papers contained a map of the school that might give him better directions and tell him where Mickey might be; he had figured that the boy might have gone to the nurse's office or the library, assuming the school had one. He'd just have to check every room he came across.

The more Christopher looked at the writing, the more unsettled he became.

F, F, F, F, F, F, F, F... My mom is going to kill me. WHY DIDN'T I STUDY?

It didn't help matters in the least that this message was written in red that was too thick to be pen, or even marker.

DO CATS EAT BATS? was repeated over several pieces of paper that were sticking out of a locker. Looking closer, Christopher though that he saw *DO BATS EAT CATS?* written a few times as well, along with pictures of bats and cats with their left eyes missing. He let it go as unimportant despite the unsettled feeling it gave him.

Some of the papers didn't make much sense at all and must have been practice for penmanship: *HS VZSBGDR.*

"Mickey? Mickey, are you here? It's me, Christopher!" he called in the hope that he wouldn't have to go much further into the school. It was so cold in the hallway. Thanks to the flashlight, Christopher could see his own breath in front of him. He wrapped his free arm around himself while the other kept the flashlight steady, scanning the hallway.

I really wish the teachers wouldn't mark wrong answers in red, one of the papers read. *It's like the paper is bleeding because they killed my answer. My answer didn't do anything wrong. It was my fault. They should kill me instead.*

Christopher shuddered.

For our senior prank we decided to lock Stanley in his locker.

The janitors will let him out.

The janitors will let him out... right?

I haven't seen Stanley in days... No one could survive that long...

I heard on the news that Stanley was reported missing.

Me too. His mom was crying and everything. The police are looking for him.

It doesn't have anything to do with us. He probably just got kidnapped or something. That happens all the time. All the time. All the time. Right? It happens all the time.

What on Earth had been going on at this school?

Hopefully, and it was a faint hope, these papers had been left by a single disturbed student, though the variety of handwriting and types of messages said otherwise.

The paper trail ended abruptly in a neat line. Christopher sent a ray of light over a locker that was devoid of papers.

Locker 317. The lock was broken. Red liquid that Christopher could only assume was blood streamed from it and puddled on the floor. He shied away from it. He didn't want to look inside. He didn't want to see what was in there. The overwhelming urge seized him anyway, and he pulled the locker door open despite his mind's feeble protests.

There was nothing but a stack of papers inside, slightly raised in the middle. He picked them up and rifled through them. He couldn't explain why—he felt like he *had* to, that there might be something important inside, no matter how horrible.

The first few drawings were stick-figure pictures of a family standing next to each other in front of a house: a mother, a father, and a child, all done in black crayon except for the robin's egg blue of the child's eyes. A typical family drawing that one might expect from a first or second grader.

Gradually, the scene changed. The dad had an angry expression on his face, then a gas can in hand. Next the house was on fire. The mom and child were crying.

Then the mom didn't have a head.

Christopher paused. He didn't really want to continue, but he had hardly made a dent in the stack of papers. He kept going, reluctant but captivated.

The next picture was a remarkably accurate charcoal sketch depicting what Christopher thought was the school. It was so detailed, it could have been done by a professional. But, it didn't look entirely like the school. If Christopher had had to guess, he would have said that it looked a bit more like...

He turned the page before he could finish the thought.

The drawings were back to stick figures, but one was scratched out. Next to it was the blue-eyed child from the previous drawings, a little bigger now. At first the figures were simply standing, just like with the family portrait. And again, it got worse.

The scratched-out figure gradually inched closer to the child, whose happy expression gradually changed to a frown.

The next few papers after that repulsed Christopher so much that he didn't even stop to look at them all. He turned them as quickly as possible, trying to avoid seeing the lewd drawings that were scribbled onto them. He almost felt bad for the paper, forced to play host to such images.

What sort of child would draw such a thing?

Finally the stick figures came to an end. What was on the next paper wasn't any more comforting.

Hello.

He turned the page.

I still think about you.

I think about you all the time.

I can't get you out of my head. I can't decide if I love you or hate you.

Why are you torturing me like this?

Why won't you come to me?

No one else thinks you're real. Can you imagine?

I know the truth.

I'm always watching you, Christopher!

Christopher threw the papers back into the locker and slammed it shut, not just because of the last message, but because of what had fallen onto the floor when he reached the end of the stack. Now he knew why the papers had been slightly raised in the middle.

Staring up at him from the floor was a cat's eye.

His vision in the dark was now just good enough to see the pupil dilate when he moved the flashlight.

Christopher backed away, hand over his mouth as he resisted the urge to throw up.

What kind of... what kind of sick, twisted person would...

As he retreated from the locker, he bumped into the row behind him. A rusty lock on one of the doors gave way, and he felt something pushing against the locker. He sprang away from it.

A body fell onto the floor.

It barely looked human, the way its skin was stretched over its bones, all of which were visible through the pale, paper-thin covering. A pair of thick glasses perched on the skull broke when they made contact with the tile.

A paper fell out with the corpse. Christopher didn't read what it said. He was too preoccupied with the fact that the body was twitching in response to the light and that its head turned toward him. Its hollow eye sockets somehow still squinted as it opened its jaw and screamed.

Christopher was down the hall before he could even register that he was moving, his body taking action when his mind could not. He slammed into the front doors but they remained firmly shut, keeping him locked inside. Behind him, the creature had managed to get to its feet.

He pushed harder against the doors, but they wouldn't budge.

"HELP!" he shouted, though he knew that no one would come.

At least he wouldn't die with his back turned. He whipped around to face the creature, flashlight raised, to find that it was nearly upon him.

When the light touched it, it let out an ear-piercing shriek and retreated back toward into dark, lashing out with nails that elongated into claws. One of them grazed Christopher's cheek, and he could feel warm blood flow from the cut and down the side of his face.

He didn't have time to worry about such a minor injury. There had to be a back door somewhere and it might be unlocked. Christopher kept his light trained on the creature and darted around it, running back down the hallway. He could hear it howling behind him, racing to keep up, but who-knows-how-many years of inactivity had weakened its legs. So long as Christopher flashed the light backward every now and then, the thing remained behind him.

Finally, Christopher reached the end of the hallway, bursting into an intersection. To his left and right there were rows and rows of classrooms that dead-ended. In front of him was a stairwell that led up to more classrooms, and possibly a fire escape.

He kept going, hardly slowing down while he considered his options. He raced toward the staircase, but suddenly shrieks emanated from above him as well. A writhing figure dragged itself down the stairs with shaky arms, all the while screeching. The noise grated against Christopher's ears.

Christopher jerked backwards, and, faced between one horrible death and another, he took the only other option available. He grabbed the handle to one of the classrooms and turned as hard as he could, praying it would open.

His prayer was answered.

The door flew open and he all but lunged through it, slamming it shut as hard as he could behind him and holding the door knob until he could hook one foot around a chair and drag it close. He jammed the chair under the knob to keep the door closed.

Thankfully there were no more nasty surprises waiting for him in the classroom, just desks covered in dust and books that looked like they had been written centuries ago and not opened for decades. On the blackboard was written, 'Classroom 317—New Student Today.'

Christopher scanned the room with his flashlight, finding that it had windows. He was only on the first floor, so he looked around for an object that would be able to break one of the panes. Then he could escape, make his way back to either the police station or Godwin's Deli, and return to the school with reinforcements.

He picked up another chair and swung it as hard as he could against the glass, but it just bounced back and sent him tumbling to the ground.

The sound of children laughing rang in his ears. He checked the room again with his flashlight, but he couldn't see anyone else, much less a group of children. When he lowered the light he heard the sound again.

"Hello? Is anyone here?"

Louder giggling answered him. Christopher got to his feet and squinted into the dark, but he still couldn't see anyone or, thankfully, anything. Yet the sound was clear, and he refused to believe, given all he had seen, that it was only in his head. He wasn't insane and he wasn't seeing things. He would not let the town's curse or conspiracy or whatever it was get to him.

"Mickey? Is that you? It's okay to come out. You don't have to hide."

The laughter continued, growing louder, closer. Christopher could see faint outlines of small children standing at their desks. They moved, circling around him, joining their hands together. Their bodies passed through the desks and chairs. The closer they got, the louder their laughing and more clear their forms.

"Hello there," Christopher said, doing his best not to sound absolutely terrified. These were the ghosts of children, he assured himself. How dangerous could they possibly be?

He aimed the flashlight to his side so he had enough light to see the children, but not so much that the brightness made them disappear from his vision. His heart ached when he took in the sight of them and saw that they weren't all there. Their uniforms were torn apart, revealing terrible burns on their arms and legs. The whites of their eyes stood out against the charred black of their skin, and what little remained of their hair was in frayed clumps. Despite the obvious pain of their condition, they all had deranged smiles plastered on their faces and were giggling still. Perhaps they had just been scared without someone to look after them and were happy to see him.

"My name is Christopher. I'm looking for someone. Can you help me?" he asked.

They continued to giggle, gesturing with their too-wide eyes to something behind him.

Christopher turned. There, in the circle of children, thicker and fleshier than the rest, was a boy he knew well. The only one not smiling.

"Mickey!" he cried out with relief, rushing away from the center of the circle to embrace the child. "Oh, thank goodness! I was so worried about you!"

The boy didn't respond.

"Mickey? Mickey, it's me, Christopher. What's wrong? I'm here to get you out of this place."

"How are you going to do that? You can't even get yourself out," Mickey said quietly. His sorrow-filled voice struck Christopher's heart sharply, not with pity like he'd felt for the injured ghost children, but with fear.

"What do you mean?"

"You have to stay here."

"Says who? Come on, let's go. We can think up a way to get home together."

The children's happy expressions didn't falter at the contradiction of their new playmate, but instead became darker. The eerie shadows dancing over their flickering forms didn't help at all.

"Christopher, listen to me. They would rather kill you than let you go. They're children. They don't know how to be selfless."

"You're a child too, Mickey."

The boy looked up. "I know."

"Mickey?"

"I'm sorry, Christopher, I really am, but I'm like them, too. I won't let you go. I can't be that selfless."

Around them, the ghost children began to chant quietly. Mickey fell silent again, though his lips mouthed the words along with the rest.

"The Dream Man is coming with his train of cars, with moonbeam windows and wheels of stars…"

"Mickey, stop this! We have to get out of here!"

"So hush you little ones, and have no fear; the man in the moon is the engineer…"

Christopher tried to pull Mickey away, but the ghosts beside him tightened their grip on the boy's hands, hard enough to make him wince in pain.

"The railroad track, it is a moonbeam bright, that leads right up into the starry night…"

Christopher looked around the circle. The expressions on the little ones' faces that had once only been creepy had become horrific. Their teeth were fangs and their hands had transformed into claws. Their eyes were deep red, their expressions ghoulish. They were turning into devils right in front of Christopher's eyes.

"So come you little ones, and run up the stairs; put on your pajamas and say your prayers…"

Christopher searched for anything he could use as a weapon, but what could he use to hurt a ghost? What wouldn't just go straight through them? Even the flashlight didn't have any real effect on them, aside from making them more translucent. Even if he was able to obtain a weapon, could he really hurt children, malevolent spirits or not?

"And ride with the Dream Man, ride with the Dream Man…"

"Mickey—"

The wicked smiles on the children's faces widened until they quite literally stretched from ear to ear. The ghosts raised their claws and approached slowly, savoring the moment. Even Mickey came forward, his eyes darker than Christopher had ever seen.

"Until daylight comes again…"

"What are you doing?" Christopher demanded frantically. "Why?"

"You can never leave," Mickey said. "You're trapped here like the rest of us."

The children giggled, though now it sounded more like sinister cackling.

"And you'll see all the wonders of Wonderland—"

"I won't," Christopher interrupted. He turned to the other children. "I won't stay here. I won't play with you."

The ghastly joy turned to rage as they snarled at him. They were next to him now, almost touching him where they stood, crowded and overlapping each other.

Christopher pulled Mickey closer to him, out of the circle, and wrapped his arms around the boy protectively. He spoke firmly, refusing to let his voice or his will waver. If he did, he had no doubt that he would be killed and spend his afterlife playing less-than-innocent games with the children. Still, he couldn't help but feel pity for them. Whatever had happened to these children to twist them so, it hadn't been their fault. Unfortunately, Christopher wasn't the person who could help them with that.

"I will not play," he said again. His tone was stern, but not mean. "It's time you all went home. Your parents will be worried sick. Don't you want to see them again?"

The children snarled; Christopher tried to cover Mickey's small body completely to shield him. He felt Mickey finally return the squeeze, and for a horrifying moment he couldn't tell if Mickey was holding him because he was afraid or if the boy was keeping him still so he couldn't run away.

Christopher closed his eyes and braced for the worst. The giggling grew louder and more menacing with each passing heartbeat. In seconds, he could feel the chill of the ghosts on the nape of his neck, then inside his body. His chest ached as if he had just run a long way in frigid air. He gasped for breath only to find himself suffocating. His nostrils stung with the smell of ash and iron.

He swayed and fell hard onto his knees. If not for Mickey, he would have collapsed on the ground.

Mickey was still holding him so tightly that Christopher felt as if his ribs were being crushed.

"I'm sorry," Christopher wheezed. "So sorry, Mickey..."

His heart missed a beat and burned. He could feel it slowing to a stop.

"It's okay, Christopher. As long as you stay here with me, I will protect you."

Finally Mickey let go, allowing Christopher to lie on the floor. His entire body was numb, yet everything hurt. Was he freezing to death, burning alive, choking, all three? His vision was swimming and he couldn't say for sure; the pressure in his chest was too heavy.

The sound of footsteps in the hall brought him back to the world of the living.

"Chris, you in here?"

"Morgan?" Christopher's voice was so faint that even he scarcely heard it. He forced his lungs to work and shouted, "In here!"

The door was shoved open and a much brighter flashlight than Christopher's scanned the room, landing on him briefly before flicking away. Morgan hurried to his side and put a hand on his neck to check his pulse.

"Chris—for goodness' sake, you're ice cold! What happened?" The officer helped him sit up. Christopher hugged him in gratitude, and to share what little warmth Morgan had. He wanted to cry and tell Morgan all the horrible things he had seen, but if Mickey saw how terrified he was, it might cause the boy to become even more scared. He must have moved aside for Morgan; Christopher couldn't see him now. The orderly asked, as calmly as possible, "How did you find me?"

"Michael told me you were looking for a kid, and I figured you might be here so I came to check. It's not safe, you know? I got worried. From the looks of it, I was right, too."

"I know. If you knew what I had been through today... I can scarcely believe it myself," Christopher said. He was reminded of the scratch he'd received near the doors and asked, "Do you have a bandage?"

"Sure, where are you hurt?" Morgan asked.

Christopher reached up to touch the side of his face where the corpse had clawed him. There should have been dried blood, if not a wound still freely flowing, but he didn't feel anything. His fingers were clean when he looked at them. Had he imagined the attack? What about the child ghosts—had he dreamed them up, too?

"How did you get in, anyway?" Christopher asked, changing the subject when he saw Morgan's concerned expression and searching eyes.

That only prompted further confusion from Morgan. "What do you mean, how did I get in? I came through the doors, like everyone else."

"But the front doors were locked, or stuck, maybe. I pushed on them as hard as I could, and they wouldn't open!"

"*Pushed*?" Morgan repeated, then burst into laughter until his face turned red.

"What? What's so funny?"

"You *pull* them open from the inside!"

Christopher stared in silence for a minute before cracking a small smile. "I was so panicked, I forgot."

"Don't worry about it, happens to all of us." Morgan looked around the classroom, a hint of wistfulness in his eyes. "This old room. Mattie and I had some good times here, way back when. Before the fire. Geez, so many kids died..."

"The hospital fire or the bridge fire?"

"Huh? No, no, though it wasn't very long after the hospital. A fire started in the school, and a lot of people were trapped inside and died. The smoke, you know. When it comes to fires, most people worry about getting burned, but breathe in too much smoke and..." He sighed. "This room in particular, even though it's on the first floor. Almost every-one in it died because they couldn't get the windows or door to open. They never did find out where the fire started, or who did it, or how, or why."

Christopher gazed around. There was indeed a layer of black soot over the desks and floor.

"So then, you and Matthew went to the hospital after that?"

"Yeah, I think so," Morgan answered, then shook his head. "No, it was before that, I think. I don't really remember. Either we were in the school fire or the hospital fire, but I don't remember which. They aren't exactly happy memories, and I don't mind that they're gone. Let's just get out of here before the whole building collapses on our heads. Can you stand?"

"I think so." Morgan rose first and Christopher took his hand, leaning on him until he found his footing. "There we go. Come on, Mickey, let's get out of here and get you something to eat."

But when Christopher turned to grab the boy's hand, he was nowhere to be found.

"**M**ickey!"

Christopher frantically searched the darkest corners of the classroom, sticking his nose into every possible crevice.

"*Mickey!*"

"What are you doing?" Morgan exclaimed in alarm. "We have to get out of here. I told you, it's not safe! We shouldn't be in here in the first place."

"Mickey is still in here somewhere! I have to find him!"

"Who?"

"I work at a children's asylum. Mickey is one of my kids, the one I came looking for. I thought he might be here, and I was right! He was with me a second ago, but now he's disappeared again. I have to find him, Morgan! He doesn't know how to take care of himself, and he's all alone, and he probably hasn't had anything to eat or drink for days! If anything happened to him, I'd never forgive myself."

Morgan placed his hands on Christopher's shoulders. "Panicking isn't going to help this situation. I'll look for him, I promise, but right now we need to get you out of here and somewhere safe so you can calm down. You've been through a lot from the looks of it, and this town has a way of getting to people."

"Please, it won't take long," Christopher pleaded. "He can't have gone far!"

"Christopher, listen to me. You're acting hysterical, and you're putting yourself in danger. I don't know what you think you saw, but you were the only one in here when I arrived. And even if he was here, don't you think he'd have left the second he could?"

The orderly wanted to protest more, but he saw Morgan's reasoning and relaxed his shoulders with a sigh. "You're right. But I still want to check. If he's alone and scared, he might not be thinking straight, and the stairs are closer than the door."

"Not thinking straight is my point exactly, Chris," Morgan quipped. Christopher was about to respond, but Morgan raised his hands. "Look, I'm not calling you crazy or anything, but I know how these old, dark places can mess with a person's head. I was serious about looking for him myself. I have a lot more knowledge about this area than you do and I know where the best hiding places are, so I'm more likely to find him. But I want you to go outside first, since you're obviously frazzled."

Christopher frowned and bit his lip. Once again, everything Morgan said was true and logical.

"You don't understand him," Christopher added, speaking calmly now, hoping it would convince Morgan that he was fine. "If you try to look for him alone, he'll run away. I'm the only person he'll talk to. Mickey is my responsibility, and I'm not going to leave him to be dealt with by a stranger."

Morgan frowned. "Alright, fine, we'll look together. But stay close. I don't want you to get hurt. You never know what's lurking in the shadows around here."

"So you do see things?" Christopher asked. He touched his cheek again. Still no blood, no pain, no anything to indicate the monster attack had really happened.

"We've all got our demons, Chris. I think you can for-give me for not wanting to talk about mine," Morgan answered. He took the first few steps up the stairs and Christopher followed in silence.

The second floor of the school was suspiciously in-nocent. No papers on the floor, no blood smears, no monsters waiting to pop out, nothing out of the ordinary.

"Mickey?" Christopher called. His voice echoed down the hallway as they waited for a reply, but no amount of yelling Mickey's name made the boy appear.

The two stepped lightly and checked each classroom. All were empty, and the accumulation of dust, soot, and a deep-seated air of regret and sorrow suggested that they had been for a long time.

For good measure, Morgan led Christopher in a thorough search of all the classrooms and offices on the first floor, too. They disturbed only a few moths.

Christopher dropped his arms to his sides and hung his head. He had been so *close*. How had Mickey managed to evade him again? For that matter, why would the boy have wanted to separate?

"One more look," he told Morgan as he returned to the classroom where he'd seen Mickey. At first it seemed nothing had changed, but when he looked at the blackboard, he noticed the writing was different. He smiled and ap-proached it. Mickey must have left him a message!

How doth the little robin bird
That flutters in his cage,
Attempt to make his voice be heard
Against bloodcurdling rage?

How quietly he waits to die
How pitiful his life,
Between horrid truth, sweetest lie
Beware the grinning knife!

It certainly wasn't the kind of message Christopher had hoped for. He would have more fondly welcomed some explanation as to where Mickey had gone. He rubbed his eyes and looked again to make sure he wasn't reading the ominous message wrong.

"Something fascinating about that old chalkboard?" Morgan asked.

That made Christopher realize Morgan couldn't see the writing. Perhaps he couldn't see Mickey, either. Maybe that was what had caused the child to disappear. "Nothing really, just thinking," he answered.

"You can think back at the station. I'll walk you over. I want to get a better look at you, make sure you didn't hit your head and get a concussion, though there isn't a whole lot I can do for you if that's the case. You might have noticed we're a little short on medical staff around here."

"I'll be alright. I've had worse," Christopher said.

Regardless, Morgan walked close to him. At first Christopher didn't notice, too preoccupied with wondering what the poem could mean. He gathered it was a warning, but there were so many dangers on the island that he couldn't begin to fathom the identity of the "grinning knife."

They were not quite halfway through the hallway when the sensation of a hand on his waist jolted Christopher far from such thoughts. He turned his head to give the officer a questioning stare.

Morgan leaned in and Christopher leaned away in perfect sync. Their faces had been so close that Christopher caught the lingering smell of alcohol in the air between them.

"You've been *drinking*? And just what are you doing, anyway?" Christopher snapped.

For a moment, Morgan looked as bewildered as Christopher felt. "I didn't have much, just a shot of bourbon. I'm not drunk or anything. And I thought, what with us having something of a moment back there, it might be a good idea to see if... I thought you were..."

"Oh, no, Morgan, no, I, uh…" Christopher stammered at Morgan's crestfallen expression. "It's not that I don't like you! It's just, now isn't a good time for me."

"Okay, okay, I got it," Morgan said, though he didn't remove his hand from Christopher's waist.

"Uh, Morgan?" Christopher cleared his throat. "Your hand?"

"Hm? Oh, yeah." Morgan still didn't move his hand. "I've been doing some thinking lately. Very lately. Just now-ish."

"About what?"

"Listen, you kind of owe me. Not only did I just sort of save your life, but you have a safe place to sleep because of me, too. So with that in mind, maybe you could—"

"I would rather not hear whatever you're going to say. The answer is 'no.'"

Morgan shrugged. "Suit yourself."

The hallway blurred and Christopher found himself pressed face-first against a row of lockers. His arms were pinned between him and the steel, and try as he might he couldn't shove himself back with enough force to push Morgan away.

"I really didn't want to do it this way. I'm not a bad guy," Morgan said. "I'm just so goddamn lonely, Chris. Don't you want to help me with that? I've been helping you. And you *said* you like me."

"Let me go!"

"*Shh.*"

Arms too strong to fight against wrapped around Christopher from behind. Cold hands rested on his hips. The smell of alcohol invaded his senses again as lips touched his neck, softly at first, then hard enough to leave a trail of bruises on his tender flesh.

The less you struggle, the less it will hurt, Christopher thought to himself. He pushed the horrible present out of his mind and focused all his thoughts firmly on where Mickey might have gone. If he could concentrate on that, he could survive this, like always.

For the second time that day, the sound of footsteps followed by the clang of metal striking metal heralded salvation. The reverberating clamor rang in Christopher's right ear, which was pressed against the locker door. He felt Morgan shift and some of the weight on his back let up, but he was still restrained.

When he opened his eyes, he saw Michael, a bloodied metal pipe, and a smashed locker.

Michael smiled his disconcerting smile at Morgan. "I didn't even swing that hard and the locker's nearly busted open. I wonder what would happen if I hit your face that hard? Harder? That would be a real shame, wouldn't it? You and Matthew wouldn't be identical anymore. And oh, look at that, your holster's empty."

Morgan's hold slackened a little more, enough for Christopher to wriggle his arms free. The orderly didn't doubt that Michael meant every word of his threat.

"Look, now," came Morgan's worried voice. "I don't want to start any trouble. What difference does it make to you, anyway?"

"I don't have to justify myself to the likes of you," Michael snarled. He struck another one of the lockers, harder this time. The door came off its hinges and clattered to the ground, a crumpled mess.

Morgan backed against the opposite row of lockers, as far from the other two as possible. Christopher wasted no time putting Michael between himself and his assailant. Michael hefted the pipe, readying it for another swing. "Now get lost."

The officer ran out of the building, still so close to the wall that his arm scraped against the lockers. Michael and Christopher remained where they were, silent until a full minute after the door had closed and plunged them into darkness.

"Thank you so much," Christopher sighed, his voice quavering. "I don't know if I can ever repay you."

"Oh, you can. But all in good time. Are you alright?"

"As alright as I can be." He shook his head. "I thought I could trust him. I don't understand why he did this. Surely he can't be *that* drunk, he was acting normal a few moments ago!"

"Morgan is an arrogant ass. He thinks no one can resist him, least of all a damsel in distress that he just rescued. He would have eventually tried to use that as leverage to make you do what he wanted. The alcohol just sped the process up." Michael wiped the sides of Christopher's face, and it was only then that he realized he was crying. "There, all better."

"You sure know a lot about this."

"I know everything."

"Right, I forgot," Christopher replied nervously. Even now, he wasn't totally comfortable around Michael. "But why follow me?"

Michael shrugged. "People like that always go after the ones they think they can dominate. It's a power thing. No offense, but you don't really look all that strong, in *any* sense of the word."

"I suppose I deserve that." Christopher rubbed the bridge of his nose between his thumb and forefinger.

"Before I forget," Michael said with a grin, "the kid you're looking for, was he wearing a yellow sweater?"

"A yellow sweater? Yes, I think he was!" Christopher laughed. He hadn't made a note of it before, but when he thought about it, Mickey *had* been wearing one. The one with the bunny rabbit stitched on the back, his favorite sweater. "You saw him, then? Which way did he go?"

"I'm sorry, I didn't really check to see which way he went. There are a lot of ways to go. It was definitely away from here, though. Anyway, I think we've waited long enough to leave. You don't really want to stay in this godforsaken place, do you?"

Christopher shook his head. "Of course not."

"We can't go back to the police station, and it would probably be a good idea to avoid the deli for a while, so why don't we go to the bar instead? You look like you could use a drink."

"I'm not much of a drinker."

"There's more than just alcohol at a bar, Christopher. And how long has it been since you had something good to drink? Besides, Morgan never goes to the bar twice in one day. It's the best way to make sure we won't run into him again."

That was a fair point.

"Alright. Let's go to the bar."

Christopher stood at the doorway to the asylum, a towel hanging over his forearm from the dishes he'd been drying only moments before. In front of him stood Madam Margot and a new child, the first newcomer since he'd begun working there. He was a little boy, not incredibly unlike the others at Woodrow: short, skinny, and not at all happy. The sun setting behind him did nothing to lighten the mood.

"This is Donald, and from now on he will be under your care. See him to his room and get him started, or whatever it is you do here."

"Oh... alright," Christopher replied. As Madam Margot stalked away, he put the towel back in the kitchen. The boy followed after him like a baby duck. Christopher extended a hand to him, but he didn't take it.

"Which room do you want?" Christopher asked as they walked by the doors. "We aren't at full capacity, but we try to have at least two people in a room. It helps for children who are afraid of the dark and things like that. Are you afraid of the dark?"

The boy shook his head.

They toured all the rooms, but the boy didn't show signs of wanting to stay in any of them, nor did he say a single word to Christopher. Without any kind of background knowledge of the child, the orderly had no idea of why that might be or how best to help him. He walked into another room and picked up a spare white rabbit plush, an old and ratty thing that was no longer soft, and offered it to the child. The boy apprehensively stretched out a hand and placed it on the rabbit, then petted its head and took it into his arms tightly.

"So, which room? Or do you want to be by yourself?" After all, maybe he was afraid of others or didn't get along well with those his own age. The little boy nodded at being alone, and Christopher led him away to the only room he knew of that had a single bed. It had been his own room for a time, but he was more comfortable in the smaller room in the North hall, where he was closer to the children and could easily reach them if they had nightmares or wet the bed.

The boy had nothing to unpack; Christopher made a mental note to get him some clothes when he next went to town for supplies. The child walked into the room, looked around, and sat on the bed quietly.

"My name is Christopher Robinson. I'm going to be taking care of you while you're here, so if you have any questions or if you need anything you can ask me. We have dinner at six, and then group therapy, bath time, story time, and bed. I hope we can become friends, Donald."

"Mickey," the boy said quietly.

"Hm?"

"My name isn't Donald. It's Mickey."

It was dark when Christopher woke up. He couldn't tell if it was night, or if it was just that dark outside from the storm clouds he had seen gathering earlier. Either way, the sound of rain hitting the window filled his ears at ten times the normal volume; his pulse did the same. He groaned, rubbing his face with one hand while he tried to gain a sense of where he was.

The first thing he noticed was the clothing on the floor.

Which, as his sluggish mind slowly came to understand, meant that he was naked.

This realization cleared some of the grogginess from his mind as he looked around. He was in a bed, covered by sheets and blankets. The room was cold and mostly empty. The only piece of furniture was the bed. The walls were white, but faded somehow, still wearing their original, now-chipping coat of paint. Christopher could see nothing beyond the window but the planks of wood that boarded it up.

What happened? he wondered, rubbing his aching forehead.

"Are you sure about this?" Christopher asked more to himself, looking up at the burned-out neon sign that read, "The Sleepy Dormouse." Now that he was standing outside, he was starting to regret his decision. Michael hadn't said much on the walk over, and what he had said only reaffirmed Christopher's earlier suspicions of him. The vagrant might have rescued him, but he was still creepy.

"Of course. You're in shock. You need to drink something and sit for a while," Michael replied, walking inside with confidence. It was Christopher's first time in a bar, and he wasn't sure what he was supposed to do, but Michael sat down on a bar stool like he owned the place and ordered a beer for himself.

There weren't any visible menus in sight, so Christopher didn't know what to order.

"How about an iced tea?" Michael suggested. "Prima makes a good one, Long Island-style. I hear it's very refreshing."

Christopher looked at Michael, then to the red-haired bartender who was eyeing him with curiosity. "Sure, that sounds good."

Prima smiled with a short laugh and set to making the tea. "I'll assume this is going on your tab, Michael?" Her voice was heavily accented, Irish or Scottish or something of that nature.

"Of course. Doesn't everything?"

Christopher felt Prima's gaze fall on him again as she placed the iced tea in front of him, waiting. He smiled at her and took a sip. It burned going down—had she put cinnamon in it?— and it didn't taste like any iced tea he'd ever had, but it would be rude not to finish it.

That's right, I went to the bar with Michael. But why does my body hurt so much? Christopher groaned, twisting experimentally in the bed and feeling aches radiate through him. *I didn't get hurt this badly at the school.*

"You sure drank that fast!" Michael laughed, only half-way done with the bottle of beer in his hand. "How was it?"

"It was..." Prima was standing right there, how could Christopher say he hadn't liked it? "Uh... interesting?" Christopher rested his head on his arm, which was sprawled on the counter.

"Feel better?"

"A little bit." He felt like his words were coming out too slow. It was hard to stay focused on any one thought. Did he feel better? More numb, maybe. That might be better.

"It must be working. I'll order you another, take this one slower."

Before Christopher could protest, Prima was already mixing up the brew. "Oh, well... okay."

Christopher sat up, and just as quickly fell back down. What had been *in* that tea? Perhaps—and he could have kicked himself for not realizing it—there had been alcohol in it after all, and this was a hangover.

After sipping away half of the second drink, Christopher was feeling talkative.

"I really owe you for helping me out back there. If you hadn't shown up when you did, who knows what would've happened," he gushed. "I was not expecting that at all! And that's someing saything. Saying something." He drowned a pathetic

sniffle with another gulp of the drink. "I liked Morgan. Why'd he have to do that?"

"Who knows? Wonderland is a strange place full of strange people." Michael's lips drew up into his usual smile. "Are you going to finish that?"

"Nah, I think I've had enough."

"Alright, in that case you had better get to bed. I find that a nice long nap usually helps me recuperate, and I doubt you've slept well in a while. You can't go back to the police station, but I know a place you can go where you'll be safe for a few hours."

"That's so nice of you! Y'know, I really should repay you for everything!" Christopher beamed. "Whad'ya say? What can I do for you? I make pretty great pancakes."

"I do have an idea..."

Oh no, Christopher thought. *I didn't! I couldn't have!*

The fact that his and Michael's clothes were on the floor and that he was in bed naked were enough to dash his hopes, regardless of the fact that Michael was nowhere to be seen. The memories he recovered did nothing to improve his mood as he struggled to find a bathroom, failed, and threw up in the hallway—partially an effect of the alcohol, partially out of disgust in himself.

"I'm such an idiot," Christopher mumbled. "I'm so *stupid!*"

Michael had even said it himself. In order to get Christopher into bed, Morgan would have seized on an opportunity to rescue him and used Christopher's appreciation to his advantage; Michael had just beaten him to it. After all, knowing Morgan as well as he did, Michael would have known he'd been drinking, if he had his gun with him or not, and what he would do. All Michael had to do was follow the sheriff, then stand back and wait a few minutes before charging in to save the day. He would have had plenty of time to find an adequate weapon. He'd even been able to predict where Christopher would be and how he'd respond, which made the orderly feel even worse. Was he really *that* easy to read?

"It's okay, Christopher Robinson."

"Mickey!" Christopher yelped in surprise and felt like he had nearly jumped out of his skin. What on Earth was Mickey doing *here*, of all places? He scoured the hallway, trying to find something to cover himself with. There was nothing. Mickey didn't seem to care.

"You were tricked, that's all. It happens to even the smartest of people," Mickey said, squatting down so he was level with Christopher, who was now curled against the wall in an attempt to hide his bare form.

"I don't think you quite understand what happened."

"Yes, I do. And it's okay."

Christopher shuddered. He didn't want to think about how Mickey had come to have knowledge of what he had just gone through. He could only hope it wasn't firsthand experience.

"Where were you, anyway?" Christopher asked, changing the subject. "Where did you go after Morgan showed up, and why did you run away? Do you have any idea how worried I've been? How *scared*? We have to get out of here, get home! Even if I have to rebuild that bridge myself, we're getting off of this island."

"That's all fine and good, Christopher, but I'm afraid it will take more than determination to leave."

The fact that he had ignored Christopher's questions was not unnoticed by the orderly. "You know more than you're telling me. You always have. Earlier in the asylum, the thing you were frustrated about and wouldn't explain to me—that had something to do with Wonderland, didn't it?"

"Yes. And even now, you wouldn't be able to comprehend it." The child looked up, as if hearing something. Christopher hadn't noticed any noise, but maybe the ringing in his ears was blocking it out. "I'm sorry, but I have to go now."

"What? No! Stay with me, please! After all this, we're finally together again, and you're going to run off alone? What are you doing, and why do you have to go? Although you probably can't tell me, anyway."

"Yes, that's right."

"Because I'm too stupid?"

Mickey wrapped his arms around Christopher's shoulders and nuzzled into his neck. Christopher returned the gesture. For a moment the monsters, the hangover, the terror, and everything else in the world disappeared, replaced by the simple joy and reassurance of a hug from someone he cared about.

"Don't worry, Christopher Robinson. You might be frightened and hurt, but you're stronger than you know. I always liked that about you."

Christopher held the boy closer. "I don't feel strong at all. Can't you stay, just a little longer? To remind me why I'm doing all this?"

"Do you need reminding?" Mickey responded, a small laugh hidden in his tone.

Christopher smiled. "No, of course not. I know why. I love you, and I won't let anything bad happen to you. Not here, not in Woodrow, not anywhere. When we get back, well... it would be hard, but if I can find another job—" Mickey seemed to hold his breath for a moment. Christopher continued. "—it's something I've been thinking about for a while now. Woodrow is no place to grow up, I know that. And if I could find a good job, and provide for you myself, and if you didn't mind, I know where the adoption papers are and how to fill out the forms. I might be able to forge Madam Margot's signature, if she would even notice. I could get all of the children adopted out, *really* adopted, and—"

"Christopher," Mickey said, cutting him off. "Do you think we can really escape from here?"

"Of course," Christopher said with the conviction of a man facing trial. "I promise, no matter what, I will find a way off this island. For your sake, if nothing else."

For a moment, Mickey almost believed him. The future that Christopher described sounded so full of hope, and he wanted it so badly. Maybe that desire, fueled by loving devotion, would actually turn into something good. Maybe there was hope.

Can we stay here a while longer, please?

CHAPTER SEVEN

*I*t must go on. It must always go on.

"Where do I go from here? How do I save you?" Christopher asked.

"Right now, I think the best chance you have at finding answers is in the amusement park. You remember where it is, don't you? And make sure you go armed. You'll be glad you did."

Christopher closed his eyes, knowing that when he opened them again Mickey would have vanished right out of his arms, the way he always did, no matter how much either of them wanted to stay together. He was starting to doubt whether Mickey was ever really there, or if he was just hallucinating. Maybe he had gone insane after all.

He was sadly proven right, to his disappointment. Why was he only right when it was about something that hurt him? He made his way back to the room, pulled on his borrowed clothing with revulsion, and checked the map in his pocket with his flashlight. If he was where he thought he was, then he was halfway between the amusement park and the rest of the town. The rain wasn't letting up.

Pulling on Michael's sweater for the extra warmth, he found the bloodied pipe abandoned on the floor and headed into the storm.

Despite the sweater, Christopher was soaked through to the bone within seconds of stepping outside the house. He couldn't see anything through the thick downpour, and the flashlight did no good at all. He could only hope he was going in the right direction. Even if he wasn't, he would just end up back in town and could wait there until the storm blew over.

The storm was fierce enough to redefine the word. Above, lightning flashed and thunder crashed as if the clouds were at war with each other. The pelting drops were so cold that Christopher was certain they were only one degree away from becoming frozen shards of hail. He could almost hear the waters of the lake threatening to swallow the island over the noise of the rain and thunder.

He put those thoughts aside. The only thing that mattered now was reaching the amusement park and taking care of whatever unknown business he had there. Mickey must have had a reason for sending him, storm or no storm, and a little rain had never hurt anybody. The rain might actually be beneficial if it drove the lurking fog monsters to find shelter and leave him alone.

Christopher dragged the pipe along the ground as he walked, smiling at the grating sound that it produced. It was malevolent, threatening; he was sure if he ever heard such a monstrous noise coming closer to him, he would flee from it, and the monsters would surely do the same. He was armed now. He could defend himself from their claws and teeth by breaking their bones before they could break his flesh.

He was alarmed. *Why am I thinking that way? Those aren't my thoughts! I don't want to hurt anyone, or anything!* But there was nothing he could do about it. The thoughts continued to come whether he wanted them to or not.

He hadn't been walking long when he spotted lights in the distance, beacons piercing the darkness and assuring him that he was indeed going the right away. He could just make out the shape of the Ferris wheel and a large, shadowy object that might have been a big top tent.

Something scraped harshly against a building to his left.

Christopher stopped, flinching away from the sound toward the opposite side of the street and raising the pipe. It was possible he might have just forgotten that he was dragging the pipe along for a second, but he didn't find that likely, nor did he think it wise to dismiss the other noise.

The rain was beginning to let up; he scanned the street with the flashlight.

Something moved!

Ahead of him, a figure vanished into an alleyway. He couldn't see what it was; the only thing that was clear was that it was several times larger than him. That was plenty enough for him to know he didn't want to meet it up close.

Christopher bolted down the street, his heavy steps sending up sprays of fallen water. At any other time, he might have been concerned about how uncomfortable his feet were, running in waterlogged socks and shoes and already sore from all the walking he'd done before, but whatever he had seen was far more important than something as trivial as coziness.

The grating sound came again; he kept running.

It wasn't long before he was out of breath. His chest ached and his muscles strained to keep going. He knew if he stopped, that thing, whatever it was, would catch up to him—and in fact, it was already gaining on him. It had been following him the entire time, and he knew it, and he knew that it knew that he knew, and he knew that it knew it could lunge forward and have him in its jaws at any time, even if he did have a weapon. It was toying with him, keeping him alive for sport the same way cats played with injured mice.

If he stopped, if he showed any sign of weakness or fatigue, there was no doubt in his mind that the monster would lose interest in the chase and attack him with whatever it was using to scrape the ground. The piercing sound became familiar, and Christopher realized it was remarkably similar to sharpening a knife, which was probably what the monster was doing. It could tear him to pieces in a few seconds. The chase was all fun and games, but when it came time to actually kill Christopher, the beast would waste no time and no effort; the kill had to be efficient.

A wild hiss erupted from the ground at Christopher's feet, causing him to lurch to the side once more. His foot slipped on the wet pavement and he crashed down, landing hard on the side that was already sore from being slammed into the lockers. His leg struck the pipe as it fell between him and the earth and pain shot through his shin, forcing a groan out of his mouth. "Ow..."

"Reowr!"

Christopher sat up slowly. The rain was just a drizzle now, but it was still dark out. If he'd had his flashlight on, he might have been able to see the outline of the black-and-white one-eyed cat that had tripped him. Christopher patted Cheshire's head in apology. A rough, pink tongue scratched the back of his hand in a signal of forgiveness.

"No hard feelings," Christopher said as he tried to stand. He winced when he put pressure on his injured leg. He was able to get back on his feet, but the most he could do was limp along the road using the pipe as a makeshift cane. Cheshire followed along beside him, occasionally mewing when there was a deep puddle in front of him before jumping over it.

For as creepy as the cat was, Christopher felt comforted by his presence and was determined to keep him close, as the sudden disappearance of the monster was apparently the cat's doing. Maybe Christopher had imagined the noise after all, and had been running all that time from nothing but his own mind's creation.

He had been doing a lot of that lately, and now that he was calmer he couldn't help but laugh. Monsters weren't real. Hadn't he learned that already at the school?

Christopher touched his cheek again for confirmation. No dry blood, no scab. Just his imagination.

He stopped as Cheshire weaved between his legs, purring and brushing against the wet fabric of his pants. Christopher stooped and picked up the cat, holding the pipe in the crook of his elbow so he could pet his furry savior.

"Who's a good kitty? You are!"

Cheshire purred and licked his cheek, and Christopher winced. It hurt more than the gentle abrasiveness of a cat's lick should. For a moment his nose burned with the smell of iron, as if a cut had been reopened.

"But what are you doing all the way out here in the middle of a storm? You have a home to go back to, you know. I bet Matthew is worried sick about you right now."

Cheshire meowed in defiance and wrestled his way out of Christopher's arms. He leapt gracefully to the ground, flicked his tail back and forth a few times as if to wave good-bye, and disappeared into the dark.

"Wait! I didn't mean for you to go back right away! Don't leave me here alone..."

Not that he was ever alone, really. He could still feel something watching him. That creeping feeling never, ever left him.

"Stop it!" he told himself.

The scraping noise returned.

He had thought that perhaps he had escaped the monster's territory, since there were no more buildings behind which it could hide—the road was now lined with trees in either direction, and the lights from the amusement park were bright and clear. Apparently, he had thought wrong.

He rolled his eyes at himself. Hadn't he *just* decided that there were no monsters on the island?

Still, Christopher readied the pipe. Whatever might be out there, he wasn't going to give up and let it kill him without a fight, and if it turned out to be nothing, then he'd only suffer a little embarrassment. He'd been through enough already and survived. Perhaps if he faced his fears head-on, he would find that he had nothing to be afraid of after all. Surely it couldn't be much worse than what he'd already experienced.

Surely it could. Cheshire had already run away. If Christopher had only been that much smarter and uninjured, he would have, too.

The rain stopped, and a few rays of weak sunlight broke through the clouds. The increased visibility did not comfort Christopher at all. He finally saw what had been stalking him through the town and into the woods, and he was very sure that even on his worst days he could not have imagined something so terrible.

From the trees emerged a gigantic abomination of a spider. Its legs, far more than eight, sprawled in all directions. Some were metal and edged in wickedly curved blades, while others were simple poles. Others still were what appeared to be the elongated humeri, radii, and ulnas of human beings, ending in long, bony fingers. Its body was covered in bristly black hairs and its face was that of a clown's, but its mouth was a mesh of rapidly clicking mandibles made of jagged steel and fangs. Some of its eight eyes were jelly-like and others were mechanical lights, but all of them glowed red.

Christopher might have fallen to his knees if he wasn't completely frozen in terror. So much for putting up a fight.

The spider let out an ear-splitting screech that turned into maniacal, high-pitched laughter. It lunged at him.

Somehow Christopher managed to move out of the way of its fangs, which he could now see were dripping with a bright green poison that made the ground hiss and bubble whenever a drop fell. He brought the pipe around to bash its head in, or try to anyway—it seemed to be made entirely of metal beneath the white face paint, and he wasn't sure his attack would be successful—but it pulled back and circled around. He wouldn't have thought something so big could move so quickly, but all those legs must be useful for maneuverability. All he knew was that if he didn't move, he would be skewered on the mass of metal spears.

The spider charged again; this time Christopher had the pipe ready, jabbing it into one of the monster's eyes. The thing howled, and at the same time Christopher let out a yell. The pipe successfully pierced the eye, causing the monster to shriek. It turned its head and shook it from side to side, all the while trying to comfort its injury with one of its skeletal appendages—but Christopher's arm caught on one of the thing's teeth and was sliced open. He began bleeding heavily. He couldn't move his injured limb. The sweater was burned away by the acidic venom that was no doubt spreading through Christopher's bloodstream, blurring his vision, causing all his muscles to seize in agony.

The pipe clattered to the ground as the monster dislodged it. Christopher would have retrieved it, but he didn't have the strength to move that far. He could barely stand.

The beast returned its gaze to him, hissing and snarling and snapping its mandibles. Its fangs again emitted the harsh scraping noise as sparks flew from the grinding metal.

Its many eyes had disappeared into only one: large, bloodshot, staring with an intensity that was all too familiar, oozing blood into the waiting mouth and onto the ground where it mixed with pools of venom. Christopher recognized the eye from the hallway at Woodrow and the hospital, and he was sure that if he had stayed longer when he had seen the cat's eye in the school, it would have appeared there, too.

It was the eye that was always watching him, the god of this hell.

Christopher's legs finally gave out and he fell to the ground, unable to move from his pathetic, prone position. He couldn't believe he was just lying on his side when a monster was hovering over him, delivering himself to it on a silver platter as if he were already dead. He was curved slightly toward his core, and he could see the blood flowing out from his injured arm, sinking into the already oversaturated earth. His head was light. He could feel his heart struggling to pump enough blood everywhere as it beat rapidly in his chest, so fast that he thought it might break through his ribs and burst right out of his body. There was pain, excruciating pain, but it felt distant now as his life faded away.

He had always thought of death as a scary thing, terrifying even, but he felt relief. No more running. No more terror. His body was already so racked with pain that he could hardly imagine the agony worsening; and if it did, it would only be briefly. Then he'd be up in the clouds singing "Amazing Grace" with all the other white-robed, white-winged angels, provided he passed his audition.

Then again, having failed to rescue Mickey, maybe he didn't deserve it.

At some point during his mental ramblings, he realized that the beast was simply watching him with that eye. It could have killed him at any point, but it hadn't. The terror that should have accompanied death was not there because—

"I'm not going to die," Christopher murmured. "You won't let me, will you? That would be too easy, too humane. I can't die, not until I'm done with whatever it is you want me to do... and then, then I'll escape from this place, and you'll regret not killing me now."

The eye blinked and again became a mesh of glowing red.

The monster screeched and sprang forward.

Christopher closed his eyes, and finally felt fear flooding back into him. Perhaps the creature had just been admiring its handiwork before finishing him off, and he really was going to die.

"Back off, this one's mine!"

Christopher looked just in time to see a flash of bright, bloody red rushing toward the monster and the glint of sunlight on steel; then his world erupted, shattered by an agonized and inhuman scream. It was, without doubt, the worst thing he had ever heard in his life.

The sound of metal grating against metal and ripping through soft flesh filled the pathway. A blur of motion whirled overhead, passing so quickly that Christopher could hardly have seen it even if his vision hadn't been suffering due to a noted lack of complete consciousness. The severed clown head tumbled forward. The spider body curled up on its back, its multifarious legs wrapped toward its center.

It twitched once, twice—then it was still.

The flash of red, now also still, revealed itself to be Prima. Her grin was wide, if not somewhat deranged. She hefted the decapitated head of the monster, which was easily more than twice her size, like it weighed nothing. She triumphantly raised an aluminum bat with the word "vorpal" written on it.

"*Callooh, callay!*" she shouted to nobody.

Then she saw Christopher.

"You're not lookin' too good there, are you?" she commented as she approached him, the head still in hand, dragging on the ground. "On the up and up, that venom'll get rid of a hangover faster than if you'd never drank in the first place!"

"It's not fatal?" Christopher asked.

"Oh, no, it is."

Christopher paled. "Is there a cure?"

"Aye. Lucky for you lad, Terceira has it."

Christopher distantly remembered Matthew describing Terceira. What the description entailed, though, was outside of his mind's frail reach. He hoped she was kind enough to give him some of the antidote.

"Is she close?"

"Aye, lives in the amusement park. Come on. I'll take you to her."

Prima pulled Christopher's uninjured arm over her shoulder to balance him as they walked. "You had a bit of a wild time last night, didn't you?" she chortled. "Don' feel too bad about it, lad. Happens t' all of us a time or two. Just not as bad." She smirked and looked down at him. "Though I wouldn't say you're a lightweight by any means. You managed to drink more than I thought you could, and you're still able to stand—mostly."

"Please, let's just hurry and get to Terceira." The poison was starting to work its way into Christopher's stomach. He didn't want to accidentally throw up on Prima's somehow-spotless scarlet boots and receive a beating from the vorpal bat. He was sure she wouldn't hesitate to send him back to death's door, even if he was ill. He wanted to talk about the events of the previous night even less.

"Not so proud of yourself, eh?" Prima quipped, laughing from her belly and hauling him along a bit more quickly. He tried to walk with her, but he found his legs were completely useless and refused to take a single step no matter how hard he willed them to move. His arms were the same way, and he couldn't feel his injured arm anymore.

Will I be paralyzed forever even if I take an antidote? Christopher wondered. The fog in his mind grew thicker, and though he could faintly hear the shrieks and howls of monsters in the woods all around them, he could not fully register them. He could barely register where he was. He remembered walking around in the forest and being attacked and Prima saving him, but sometimes when he closed his eyes he mistakenly believed he was back on the road from the asylum to the town of Woodrow to fetch supplies, having decided to walk and get help since he couldn't move the tree branch that was blocking the way.

In his clearest moments, he could hear Prima faintly humming a tune that sounded oddly familiar. As she hummed, he tried to follow along, mumbling the words sluggishly.

"The Dream Man is coming with his train of cars, with moonbeam windows and wheels of stars... So hush you little ones, and have no fear; the man in the moon is the engineer..."

He remembered it now. It was a nursery rhyme, one of the children's favorites to hear before bed. They said it gave them good dreams. Christopher doubted it would afford him the same luxury as darkness overtook his vision.

> *"... 'One, two! One, two! And through and through*
> *The vorpal blade went snicker-snack!*
> *He left it dead, and with its head*
> *He went galumphing back.*
>
> *And hast thou slain the Jabberwock?*
> *Come to my arms, my beamish boy!*
> *O frabjous day! Callooh! Callay!*
> *He chortled in his joy.*
>
> *'Twas brillig, and the slithy toves*
> *Did gyre and gimble in the wabe;*
> *All mimsy were the borogoves,*
> *And the mome raths outgrabe.'"*

"Read it again, read it again!"

Christopher laughed; this was the third time he had repeated the poem, and there was no question that it was a favorite. "I'm sorry, children, but it's time for bed."

One-and-a-half-dozen disappointed groans reached his ears as he closed the book he'd been reading—Through the Looking-Glass—and placed it back on the shelf. There were not too many books on it, which always made him a little sad, but at least they had Alice's Adventures Underground, a collection of Grimm's Fairytales, and a few Westerns.

"We'll read more tomorrow. For now, you all need to get some sleep. It's good for you."

"But Mr. Christopher!"

"No 'buts'."

He saw each of the children to their rooms and tucked them in. Christopher was somewhat relieved that the asylum was not filled to its capacity, but the children often imagined things on the spare bunks that gave them nightmares.

A few of the children fell asleep almost as soon as their heads touched their pillows. Others cuddled with their undressed dolls or mangy stuffed animals that were falling apart at the seams. Christopher wished that Madam Margot would spare some money to give them new toys. He wasn't sure most of the current toys would survive another wash, and he didn't have the sewing skills needed to fix them up. Or a needle and thread, for that matter.

Soon enough, all the children were snug in bed, fast asleep without him even having to sing them their lullaby. The poem had served that purpose just as well.

By the time he had finished attending to the other children and made his way back to the game room, Mickey—who had bravely ventured out of his room on the other side of the asylum at Christopher's insistence—was already fast asleep on the blanket the children had been sitting on moments before. Christopher sighed, smiled a soft, fond smile, and he lifted the boy up.

Mickey responded to the sudden movement by wrapping his arms tightly around Christopher's neck to make sure he wouldn't fall. Mickey opened one bleary eye, saw the familiar face, and went back to sleep, nestled under his caretaker's chin. It was a shame, really; Christopher had wanted to ask what he'd thought of story time and if he might want to join the other children in more activities. There were group therapy sessions and movie night, when Christopher would bring the black-and-white television and VCR out of storage and play a Disney movie, or anything else child-friendly that he could find in town. It took a lot of convincing to get Madam Margot to splurge on such a luxury. He had to save up for new videos by the cent, but it was something the children really enjoyed, and Christopher couldn't blame them.

Those questions would have to wait until morning. Christopher carried Mickey down the west hall, all the way to the end, and settled him into his bed. He tucked him in gently and was almost out of the door when he heard a small, "Christopher Robinson?"

He turned back to the child. "Yes, Mickey?"

"Good night. I love you."

"I love you, too," Christopher replied with a smile, but the boy was already sound asleep.

He hated clowns. HATED them.

It was the face paint, he thought. The way it concealed their true expressions and made them something not-quite-human unsettled him, and he could never relax around them. When they were on stage performing was one thing. Encountering one outside of its act was entirely different.

He'd already found Anderson, Ray, Caitlin, and Thea, and they had assured him that the only other missing child was Mickey; since he hadn't spotted anyone else out of bed after Sarah had come to tell him they had snuck off, he trusted their word on that.

"Mickey!" he called. "Where are you? Come here!"

Christopher was frantic. A circus had set up on the edge of Woodrow and the children wanted to see it, but Madam Margot wouldn't let them go. That wouldn't stop the hyper ones, though Christopher didn't understand how they'd managed to talk Mickey and Thea into going with them. Perhaps Mickey, now finally beginning to open up, had wanted to impress the other children by going along for the ride.

Cackling laughter reached Christopher's ears and he moved toward it, the children now obedient ducklings following behind him. The laughing led him away from the big top and toward the trailers where the circus staff ate and slept.

A group of clowns surrounded a small, quivering form. Fury surged through Christopher and he charged over. He didn't give a single thought to the fact that he was outnumbered or that he'd never been in a fight in his life. In reality, the clowns had most likely been trying to make the child laugh and had accidentally scared him in the process, but in Christopher's mind *they were tormentors and one of his precious little angels was in danger.*

"Get away from him!" he shouted, and they retreated a few steps from the trembling form that latched onto Christopher as soon as he was close enough. He could feel the tears falling on his shirt and the rough tremors that shook Mickey's body as the small boy tried to press every part of himself as close to Christopher as possible.

The clowns sneered, still laughing at the traumatized child in his arms.

Christopher glared, unable to put into words all the things he wanted to say—especially not with children present—and walked back to the car. With Mickey on his lap, they were all able to squeeze in. They returned safely to the asylum and were in bed before dawn. Madam Margot was never any the wiser.

From that day on, Mickey hadn't wanted to spend any time with the other children. He only left his room to use the bathroom, and never for longer than absolutely necessary. He refused to talk to anyone other than Christopher. Even when he did speak it was far less often, with far fewer words than he had used before. Most of their conversations consisted of Christopher trying to coax the boy out of his shell and Mickey stubbornly turning down any activity that would require him to leave the confines of the West Wing. When it wasn't that, it was Christopher calming Mickey after he'd had a nightmare or a panic-inducing flashback.

All the progress that Mickey had made was dashed in a single night.

He hated *clowns.*

"Wake up! We're here."

The amusement park was sealed behind high, rusty gates. They sported barbed bars at the top to dissuade the rowdier crowd from climbing over after hours. Bits and pieces of a thick chain and padlock poked out of the dirt. If Christopher had been more detail-oriented after having been jerked out of his brief slumber, he would have wondered if Prima had destroyed the lock with the bat, or if she'd taken a chainsaw to it instead. She certainly seemed the type to be enthusiastic about such things.

He tried to get up and walk but instead had to be dragged in, barely conscious. His body was in agony, and though his mouth hung open and his face was twisted in pain, he could not scream or even beg Prima to move faster. He fought for control of his bowels and tried his hardest not to lose their contents; thankfully, he succeeded in this.

Even with his eyesight still blurred and his mind barely functioning beyond the capacity to recognize pain, he was able to comprehend the park's state of utter disrepair. The rides were completely rusted over (not that he had expected anything different) and the pathway was filled with puddles, worn down and crumbling from years' worth of erosion and harsh weather. Some of the attractions were boarded up; others simply stood, forlorn and menacing, glaring at the two while they passed. Posters that had once brightly displayed the features of the park were so faded and had bled so badly that they were illegible, their subjects horribly deformed and unrecognizable even by the standards of a freak show.

Christopher had no love for the park and no idea why Mickey would send him to such an awful place. Everything about it was decrepit, and as soon as he got the cure for the poison and discovered what it was that Mickey meant for him to learn there, he would leave and never look back.

Prima brought him to the big top tent. Inside, the seats were clear of fallen popcorn and sticky soda spills—it was neat and well-maintained, unlike everything else in the amusement park. Terceira had to do something with her time, Christopher supposed, and if this was where she lived then she would want it to be tidy. In the center of the arena was a long table set with all kinds of food that he probably would have drooled over in other circumstances. However, in his current situation, all it did was make him heave up bile.

"Pansy," Prima remarked. She hauled him to the table and shoved him into a seat at one end. He could make out the vague silhouette of another woman dressed entirely in green at the other end. Her face was covered in a veil, so Christopher couldn't tell what she really looked like.

Prima grabbed a bottle off of the table and thrust it into Christopher's face, making him recoil and retch at the smell.

"Drink this," she commanded. Christopher forced his mouth open and took a gulp. He had to fight not to spit it back up the second he tasted the alcohol, and it only made him feel worse. Despite his struggling, he coughed the liquid onto the ground.

Before he could catch his breath, Prima snatched the bottle from his hands and shoved it at him again. "Come on, I've seen you handle more than this."

Christopher shook his head and covered his mouth with his hand. "I don't want to drink that stuff again!"

"You have to if you don't want to die!" Prima snapped. "Alcohol counters the poison. Drink, or I'll make you."

"You'll have to make me, then."

Foolish words from a foolish man.

Prima battled with Christopher much like she had with the spider, beating him into submission without mercy. Once she had him pinned down (which was no difficult feat), she pinched his nose so he had to open his mouth to breathe. The second after he inhaled, she shoved the bottle into his mouth. Once she thought enough of the liquid had poured out, she forced his jaw shut, still keeping his nostrils closed so he had to swallow.

Prima stood, leaving Christopher to sputter on the ground and try to get the burning sensation out of his throat and nose. He hated the taste and the feeling, but he had to admit that his arm didn't hurt as much. Then again, that might just be the general numbing effect of the alcohol he'd just been made to drink.

At some point during his scuffle with Prima, the woman in green had risen from her seat and come to stand at his side. She glanced at his arm, then wrapped a bandage around the wound to stop the bleeding.

"Now that's over with, introductions are in order. Terceira, this lad is Christopher. You remember him, I'm sure," said Prima. He didn't manage to ask what she meant by that, as he was sure he'd never met Terceira, before she went on, "Christopher, this is my lovely wife, Terceira."

"Wife?"

"Yeah, what's it to you?" Prima responded sharply. "If you've got a problem with it, then you best keep it to yourself. And don't even think about hitting on her, or I'll bash your head in. Understand?"

"No, ma'am—I mean, yes, ma'am!" Christopher said. He hadn't meant to be rude. He was only surprised at Prima's boldness, though perhaps he should not have been, given her overall demeanor.

Terceira giggled at Prima's comment and Prima cracked a smile once more. "Your laugh is so cute, dear."

"This is the one from the bar last night?" Terceira asked, gesturing to Christopher. Her voice was soft and quiet, the polar opposite of Prima's. She smoothed a lock of hair out of Christopher's eyes. "Oh, you poor thing!"

"He'll be fine," Prima assured her, placing a hand on the smaller woman's shoulder. "He's tougher than he looks, if he made it all the way here."

Christopher could just barely see Terceira smiling beneath her veil. "Hopefully not too tough."

Prima clapped her hands. "Let's eat, then—and I expect you to clear half the table, Christopher. You're dehydrated and haven't been eating enough as it is."

Christopher looked over the spread. He didn't recognize any of the food that was being served. He might not have eaten many gourmet meals in the asylum, but he would surely be able to identify different types of meat, and the entire banquet seemed to be nothing but meat.

Maybe it's from a different country? he wondered. *Somewhere women can marry women—and men can marry men?* He thought of Morgan, then Michael, and found his appetite further soured. *What did I do to make them attack me?*

Prima handed him a fork and knife and pushed a plate toward him. It was piled with something that looked like ham, maybe, after the meat was taken off and the bones could be seen, but it was a deep red. Like a tomato, or something less appetizing, and it had the consistency of frozen gelatin that had only just begun to thaw. Christopher poked it with his fork and it jiggled in response. When he looked up, he saw Prima staring at him expectantly, and he presumed that, beneath her veil, Terceira was, too.

"Terceira worked hard on this meal. Don't be rude," Prima said.

He cut off a piece and put it in his mouth, even though he really wasn't hungry after his latest ordeal and he just wanted to lie down and sleep for the rest of his life. When he chewed, the meat-stuff bounced back against his teeth like rubber. It was quite a few minutes before he was able to swallow his single mouthful, and even then it settled in his stomach thickly.

He honestly couldn't say what it tasted like. It wasn't like anything he had ever eaten. The closest thing would be the bacon he'd had in his sandwich at Godwin's Deli, though this was not quite the same.

It wasn't bad—quite the opposite, actually. Despite its foreign texture, he found himself craving another bite and he took one, smaller this time so he wouldn't have to chew as long. The more he became accustomed to the gelatinous nature of the stuff, the more he found it to his liking. Each bite was better than the last, and it gradually became easier to chew.

By the time he was halfway through his plate, and thoroughly surprised that he had eaten so much, Christopher glanced at Prima and Terceira and noticed that they hadn't touched a single thing on the plates in front of them. Almost immediately he set his fork and knife down.

"I'm sorry. Was I supposed to wait?" he asked sheepishly, though he felt far more like a pig.

"No, no. You just seem like you're enjoying yourself, that's all. How is it?"

Christopher looked at the red mass. "It's delicious."

"Thank you. It's an old family recipe," Terceira said.

"You've never really had anythin' like it before, have you lad?" Prima laughed. "'S alright, too. It's not somethin' most people come 'cross in their lifetimes."

"What is it? If that's okay to ask, I mean. I know people can be protective of their recipes, but I like this so much I can't help but be curious."

Prima chuckled. Terceira's head tilted back slightly as if she too were laughing, but no sound escaped through the veil.

"You just eat up and get strong, lad! You'll need it to survive. There's worse things than the Jabberwock wanderin' around these parts."

"Monsters, you mean?" Christopher asked, intrigued. If Prima and Terceira had any information on how to escape the town, or why it was the way that it was, then that might be why Mickey had told him to come here. This would bring him one step closer to their salvation.

And, he had to admit, he found solace in the fact that the spider-clown had been undeniably real. He wasn't insane after all, and if Prima knew much about it, then she would know about the other monsters he had heard and seen, too.

Prima looked at him with all seriousness and she answered with an edge in her voice, "Aye. Monsters."

"Worse than that thing? The Jabberwock?" Christopher assumed she meant the mechanical clown-headed spider, the one whose head was now at her feet like a deformed dog begging for scraps next to the table.

"Aye, there are. You should know, lad, one of 'em took you home last night."

Christopher jumped up from his seat angrily. "How dare you—!"

"Calm down, lad." Prima shrugged. "We've had our own problems with men, haven't we, dear?" Terceira tilted her head solemnly toward her plate. "You're in good company, Christopher."

"Oh, I... I'm sorry," Christopher said, though his face still burned with embarrassment. "What's wrong with Michael, anyway? He's creepy, I'll admit—and he did take advantage of me—but I think I would still take him over the Jabberwock, or any of the other monsters I've encountered. At least he didn't try to kill me."

Prima's laughter was cold and harsh this time. "Lad, you know nothing of Michael."

"You're right, I don't. Why don't you enlighten me?"

"There's too much to know," Prima sighed. "All you need to know is that Michael is worse than all of the other monsters here. Much worse. This island is a web, and he's the spider."

"Then you mean, he's behind all of this?" Christopher leaned forward. "He brought me here? And Mickey?"

"All of us," Prima answered.

"But how?"

"You're better off not thinking about it too much. Better off here with the three of us."

"Three?" Christopher asked.

"Yes. Me, Terceira, and Abel."

"Abel? He's here, too?" Christopher looked around, but didn't see anyone else. Was he hiding in the stands? Perhaps he was washing up before dinner, but it was certainly taking him a long time to reach the table. Christopher should have waited after all, if all the guests weren't seated.

Prima cackled in a way that could only be described as maniacal, with her head tossed back and her face pointed straight up at the ceiling. Her mouth was wide and her torso shook with the force of each erupting squeal.

Terceira lifted her head. "It's an old family recipe," she repeated.

Christopher stared across the table again, surveying the food. A lot of it suddenly looked familiar. Like something he had seen once in a book about human anatomy.

He nearly retched, but his body was so starved for the nourishment it had lost, it refused to cooperate with him. It kept the contents of his stomach firmly intact now that he didn't want them.

"Oh, no..." he whimpered.

Prima and Terceira rose from the table, their knives in hand.

Christopher grabbed his own knife, turned, and ran out of the big top tent as fast as his legs would take him.

♣ *CHAPTER EIGHT* ♣

Christopher's legs felt like lead. His stomach was filled with dead weight. He was too tired from the ravages of poison and weak from the effort it had taken his body to expel the toxin.

Prima's cold, cackling laughter echoed behind him, in front of him, all around him, *followed* him. The amusement park was her territory, and he knew nothing. He couldn't even place the attractions that he had seen on the way in, given the fact that he'd been half-delirious then and was still dizzy now. The two women would know where he was going to hide before he even found a place he thought was suitable.

The rain had started up again, just a drizzle, but with the promise of a real downpour. Christopher didn't like the prospect of staying out in the rain, especially when he didn't dare use his flashlight. He reached for the light on instinct, only to realize that his pockets were empty. The only thing he still had was the table knife. He must have dropped the flashlight somewhere in the woods during the struggle with the Jabberwock.

What good would the little knife do when Terceira had her own and Prima was probably wielding the bat again? He would either have to find a better weapon to defend himself with or get out of the amusement park. As it was, he couldn't remember the way out. He was at a high risk of bumping into one of the cannibals while he was running around like a scared rabbit looking for the exit.

He found a deep fold in the fabric of one of the tents and pressed himself into it, his cheek scraping against the tarp. At least it was dark, and if he was still and silent, he might just disappear into it and escape his hunters' notice. If only he had the time to stop and think of what to do next, or come up with a better idea than hiding in the fold of a tent.

Suddenly the whole world was lit up like a summer day. As if they had read his thoughts, Prima and Terceira had turned on the power for the entire amusement park. The flash of lights and blare of music made him jump, and he took off at a dash to find better cover. In the distance, but not nearly distant enough, he could hear Prima's crowing.

"Come out, come out, wherever you aaare!"

Christopher clung to the side of the nearest solid building and focused on his breathing.

In, out. In, out. In, out.

"Here Chrissy, Chrissy, Chrissy!"

In, out. In, out. In, out.

"I know you're heeere, Christopher!"

In-out, in-out, in-out.

The sound of splashing filled his ears.

In-out-in-out-in-out-in-out...

He turned the corner and ducked into the building.

Inside, the dripping of rainwater plinked through the darkness. The building must have been connected to a different circuit from the other attractions, as the lights—assuming there were any—had not turned on. Christopher moved forward to search for the heart of the darkness. That was where he was least likely to be found until he could come up with a coherent plan to escape back to town without being killed by Prima and Terceira, or the monsters that no doubt infested the woods around the park.

Christopher had hardly taken three steps before he smacked painfully into a wall. He stumbled backward and rubbed his aching nose, using his other hand to feel his way forward. Groping about in the dark wasn't something he was especially confident about or eager to do, but he didn't have any other choice. He crept along with one hand on the wall to steer himself clear of any obstacles that might cause him or his nose further damage.

After wandering around for a few minutes, he sat on the floor and drew his knees to his chest, trying to think. All he had to do was put his hand on the wall and walk the other way to get out, but what would he do then? Prima and Terceira wouldn't give up their search easily; they would find him long before they tired of the sport or he came close to escaping. No one would think to look for him, and even if they did, what could they do? Prima and Terceira had already killed and eaten Abel, and there was no doubt in Christopher's mind that they'd do the same to everyone else who dared trespass in their domain.

This is hopeless, Christopher thought. *But everything else so far has been hopeless too, and I'm still alive.*

"Christopheeer? Are you in heeere?"

He stopped breathing. Stopped thinking. He tried to stop his heart from beating, sure that Prima would hear it pounding in his chest. The way her voice was echoing in the room, he couldn't tell which direction it was coming from or how far away she was.

"Hmm... the floor's wet," Prima went on. "And it's dark in here. Let's turn on the lights! Eyes shut or you'll go blind!"

Even with his eyes closed, the brightness of the lights seared through his eyelids and he had to cover his eyes with his hands. He almost didn't want to move them. If he could hide like that, prevent himself from seeing anything, maybe it would all go away.

But then who would rescue Mickey?

Christopher waited a moment until his eyes had adjusted to the light, then forced them open. He could finally see what filled the room.

Monsters.

They surrounded him, their too-wide mouths agape and moaning silently in what might be agony... or possibly the pleasure of knowing there was prey within easy reach. Their claws stretched forward expectantly, hungrily. Most of them clambered to where Christopher was now utterly frozen, their limbs jerking and twitching inhumanly. Others kept their distance and wandered aimlessly without eyes, ears, or a nose to tell them that he or anything else existed. Behind them, he glimpsed the shock of red hair from the Jabberwock's clown head, now reattached to its mangled mess of a body.

With the realization that he was not being devoured alive came another: the monsters were pressed against something that would not allow them to go further, making them unable to reach him.

Mirrors, he thought. *The lights are on behind the mirrors so I can see what's on the other side.* He was pretty sure some trick mirrors could work that way.

If he was going to run, now would be the perfect time. Prima couldn't see him, but the dim light behind the mirrors illuminated the shadowed path enough for him to find his way out. All he had to do was run between the monsters. Slowly, he forced strength back into his stiff and trembling legs and stood, placing a hand on the side of the mirror.

The monsters responded to his movements and followed him, howling inaudibly behind the thick glass and slamming their bodies against it, making it shudder with such force that more than once Christopher thought it might give way and allow them to devour him. He doubted that they could see him—most likely they were simply following the sound of his footsteps and breathing.

He got a good look at them. He saw now that none of them had eyes; rather, their skin had melted together where their eyes should have been. Their noses were pointed up and hooked, not unlike some species of bats. That was where the similarities between each of them ended. Every abomination had its own unique distortions that made each of them individually terrifying. Christopher was sure that, if they'd all looked the same, his mind might have been able to process it and help hold the terror at bay, but he had to continually adjust to fresh frights.

One beast that had two heads and no arms rushed into the wall hard enough for one of the skulls to crack and ooze black blood. Christopher leapt backwards, losing his knife and his connection to the glass wall.

The lights went out.

When he reached to find the wall again, he touched nothing but empty air. He didn't dare crouch down and feel around for the knife; he feared he would not find the courage to rise again. As it was, he could barely stay standing.

"Did you enjoy our sideshow?" Prima laughed. "You see, each of the monsters on this spit of land is different. That's what makes it so difficult to collect all of them."

The lights changed, flaring in front of the mirrors now. Christopher was dazed as his eyes burned, painfully adjusting to the sudden, sharp brightness. He hadn't had warning and was stunned for a moment.

When he was able to open his eyes again, he saw dozens of himself reflected in the mirrors, which meant Prima knew without a doubt he was there. She probably also knew where in the maze he was—and that was much, much scarier than the monsters had been.

And for some reason, his reflections were wearing the white collared shirt and sweater vest he'd worn when he left the asylum. But that couldn't be right. He was wearing Michael's sweater now, wasn't he?

A glance down proved him wrong. He was wearing the sweater vest and shirt that he had abandoned in the police station. Come to think of it, the clothes strewn about on the floor of the bedroom hadn't been the borrowed uniform he'd been wearing, either.

This is no time to think about that, you idiot! Focus on escaping!

His reflections looked around as he did, some back at him, some off in other directions, all with a bewildered and fearful expression that made him almost ashamed. After all he had been through, surely he should be able to handle this. The monsters were locked away. They couldn't hurt him if they tried, and they already had. This time, his enemy was a human. A human who was a cannibal and had single-handedly defeated gigantic monsters, but a human nonetheless. A human who could be outrun and outwitted.

He pressed his hand to the closest mirror and began to run. He could do this. He *had* to do this. Mickey was depending on him!

Terceira's voice joined Prima's. Christopher didn't think they were talking to him now, but instead exchanging a sing-song poem. First Prima would sing a line, then Terceira sang back to her, their voices resonating and echoing so Christopher had no idea where they were. More than once he changed direction in an effort to avoid them, unsure if he had succeeded, and he was beginning to lose track of where he'd been trying to go.

"Oh, cook the man up, dearie, cook the man up,
For you, love, cook the man up!
Oh, cook the man up, dearie, cook the man up,
Give me some thyme to cook the man up!

As I was walking down Jabberwock Street,
For you, dear, cook the man up!
I happened across a most succulent meat,
Give me some lime to cook the man up!

So I took him home to my lovely wife,

It was one thing for them to plan to eat him, but Christopher felt it was rather rude to sing about how they were going to do it on top of everything else.

The lights changed, revealing the dungeon of monsters once more. Prima was most likely controlling the switch, so she had to be near the generator. The direction of her voice varied due to Christopher moving further from and closer to her, not because *she* was moving. That meant it was Terceira who was most likely roaming the hallways with him. He had seen how ruthless Prima was when she had faced the Jabberwock, and it was hard not to be relieved that she wasn't trailing him. On the other hand, Terceira might be worse.

And that was assuming the lights weren't automated.

He picked up his pace, trying to keep out of their reach, yet he had no way of knowing if he was running away or running right toward them. Even if he hadn't been disoriented coming in, this mirror maze was impossible to navigate. The exit could have been right in front of him or miles off, and he wouldn't know the difference.

Again the lighting changed, concealing the monsters and revealing his location.

He came face-to-veil with Terceira. His heart plummeted into his stomach at once as he sprawled backwards, but it was too late. She had seen him.

Christopher had been mistaken in thinking that she was armed with a knife. Instead, Terceira carried a chainsaw, the chain of which was studded with real human teeth that had been sharpened to perfect, deadly points.

Beneath the veil, he could see her offer him a thoughtful smile, like she was wondering what he would taste like with lime juice and thyme sprinkled over his flesh.

"Why are you doing this?" Christopher demanded. If he'd had the capacity to think clearly, he might have been startled by the force in his usually quiet and uncertain voice. "What do you have to gain by killing me?"

"Absolutely nothing." Prima appeared behind Terceira. She had the vorpal bat in her hand, just as Christopher had expected, though he was surprised she had arrived so quickly. The generator—and the exit—must be close, if his hunch was right. He might be able to make a run for it. "There's nothing left to gain anymore. Not here."

"You're ill," Christopher said, trying to sound reasonable. "Maybe I can help you. We can talk this through."

"If anyone needs help, it's you." Prima's mouth stretched from ear to ear in a wide grin. Christopher's burst of courage began to wane. "Do you not understand yet? This place is our punishment for our wicked lives, and the island is only appeased by bloodshed and madness. The more you resist, the worse it will be for you."

"Speak for yourself!" Christopher snapped. "I'm not mad, and I'm not wicked!"

"Are you sure?"

The fact that Terceira's softer voice soothed him was the most unsettling aspect of her question. He had expected her words to gain the same maniacal edge that Prima's had, but her tone remained as genial and mouse-like as ever. She was calm in her homicidal lunacy.

She had a point. Hadn't he been having the most horrible thoughts lately, violent thoughts?

No, those aren't mine.

"Yes," he said evenly, "I'm sure."

"Then you've forgotten, and that's the worst crime of all," Prima replied.

Christopher glared at her, surprised by the superiority in her voice. As if *he* was the villain, the one who could not be tolerated, the one who had done as horrible a thing as kill and eat Abel, or assault someone who was afraid and vulnerable, or take advantage of someone's trust. His hands were clean, he was sure of it.

"I'm not wrong. I'm not a criminal."

"You have done wrong," Terceira said, almost as if she was genuinely trying to help him remember his transgression. "We all have, or else we wouldn't be here."

"And what is it that I did? What could I have done to land me here?"

"Who have you let down, Christopher?"

The accusation shocked him into silence. Mickey had sent him here, after all. He didn't want to hear it from these two, but if they had information about the boy, this traumatic visit might just be worthwhile after all.

Before he could say anything, Prima clicked her tongue like a mother scolding a child and swung the bat around once to steady her grip on it.

"I suppose it can't be helped, but it doesn't much matter now. Things will return to normal once we kill you. No more of this poking around and asking questions that shouldn't be answered. We can all get back to business as usual. It's your fault that all these things are happening, that all these new monsters are appearing and everyone's going mad again. It happens every time you show up."

"How should we prepare him?" Terceira asked. "I was thinking that a nice pot roast would warm the tent after this rainy weather."

"As long as it isn't stew, darling, I'll eat anything you cook."

"Alright." Terceira smiled, turned on the chainsaw, and revved it. Her voice was barely audible over the noise of the thing. "Off with his head!"

The lights went out.

Christopher turned on his heel and ran, not caring to keep his hand against the mirror. Once more he couldn't see where he was going; he only knew the chainsaw was roaring behind him, close but not gaining.

He crashed into corners of invisible, mirrored turns more than once, colliding against the glass with his shoulders, but the adrenaline coursing through his veins blocked out the pain and kept him running. His legs moved faster and faster as the world slowed around him, and yet he felt as if he hadn't moved an inch.

The lights came on. One blink to adjust was all Christopher had before he was running amidst the distorted freaks. They swarmed over each other like ants over a dead bird in their haste to follow him. They never doubled back to Prima or Terceira, so he had no idea where the women were now. The monsters stayed trained on him; the stench of his fear must have been as attractive to them as a budding rose.

If not for the noise of the chainsaw, Christopher might have believed that he had outrun the killers and reached safety... as if safety were anything but a foolish dream, both in the tainted circus and out of it. But at least he knew where the outlines of the pathway were. Soon the lights would change again, revealing Christopher's reflections and the edges of the mirrors, and the path would stay lit.

The building hadn't looked big from the outside. Surely he didn't have far to go before he came out the other side, and then he could find somewhere else to hide. Maybe he could even climb over the fence and flee into the forest. He regretted not trying to dodge past Terceira and Prima to the exit that had probably been right behind them. The prospect of running himself into the saw or the bat had not been attractive, but attempting it might have saved him from getting lost again.

He could almost taste freedom on his lips, just like one of Matthew's sandwiches. He would go back to Godwin's Deli, tell Matthew what had happened, have something to eat or drink while the deli owner called his twin. Morgan wouldn't refuse a call for help from his brother, and Morgan would bring a gun. Not even an aluminum bat or a chainsaw had any hope against a gun.

Once Christopher was safe again, he would stay in the comfort of the deli, rather than blindly venturing into the belly of the beast. He would focus on trying to find Mickey and figuring out why he was in this horrible town.

Everything would be fixed. Everything would be alright.

His legs flew out from under him and he hit one of the mirrors hard before collapsing on the ground. His left leg and hip screamed as pain shot through his bones. It wasn't the first time he'd had a hard landing, but this one felt much worse, especially given it was the second time in the same day. He didn't think the leg was broken, but it might as well be—he wasn't going to be getting up again before Prima and Terceira found him, and it wouldn't be long before they did.

The light changed once again, as he had anticipated. His form was everywhere, showing his face contorted in pain. In a moment, he understood that this time, he hadn't fallen down. Prima had caught up and struck his leg with the bat, so it probably was broken after all.

It took longer for his mind to process this, since neither Prima nor Terceira—who now loomed over him—appeared in the mirrors. Christopher's mind fumbled for an explanation of this newest phenomenon, found none, and focused instead on the fact that he was again on death's doorstep. This time he was sure his knocking would be answered.

Yet, the women weren't moving.

When Christopher looked at his pursuers, they were both frozen in fear, shaking, staring at something behind him. Prima dropped her bat. The motor of Terceira's chainsaw cut out and died.

Christopher looked over his shoulder.

The reflection in the mirror nearest to him wasn't his. Instead, he saw Michael's forbidding, smiling face. His eyes were flickering with the same madness that glowed in Prima's; the corners of his mouth twitched in rage even as he grinned. Christopher instinctively dragged himself away from the image and found a corner to curl up in while he nursed his injured leg.

"We weren't really going to hurt him, honest! We know he's yours!" Prima yelled, as if the volume of her statement would make it true. "Just a game! A little game of cat and mouse! We were having fun, weren't we, Chris? Tell him!"

Terceira made something that sounded like a squeaking noise, but it was so faint that Christopher couldn't be sure.

The lights went out again.

For a moment, everything was silent.

Footsteps, slow and steady—too much so for them to belong to a fleeing Prima or Terceira—echoed through the hall of mirrors.

For what felt like forever, there was no other noise.

Then it started.

The revving of the chainsaw threatened to deafen Christopher, followed immediately by horrible screaming that stabbed straight into his core and tore him up inside. The room wasn't dark enough; his eyes had adjusted to the shadows and he could clearly see Prima and Terceira's outlines.

Although Prima and Terceira had been about to kill and eat him, he felt pity for them. Being slowly dismembered was an excruciatingly painful death. Come to think of it, he was probably next. At least the women had intended to cut his head off first so he wouldn't feel the rest of the butchering. Who knew what Michael would do to him?

Especially given what Michael had already done to him.

He brought his knees closer to his chest, lowered his forehead onto them to hide his eyes, and put his hands over his ears to block out the noise and his own thoughts. It was a futile effort against the ladies' soul-piercing hysterics as they were torn apart. Even if he closed his eyes and hid them, he could not shake the images from his mind. He would hear those screams and be haunted in his dreams by the sight of their mangled bodies forever.

After what seemed like hours, the agonized chorus of shrieks and yells ended, and so did the noise of the chainsaw. The lights came on behind the glass. The monsters were still there, writhing with each other. This time they ignored Christopher and swarmed to the glass separating them from the mass of unidentifiable body parts and ocean of blood that had once belonged to their captors. Michael was nowhere to be found, and Christopher wondered if he had ever really been there. The chainsaw lay just out of his reach, but he had no desire to pick it up.

He shuddered, hating himself for having looked at their remains. He couldn't bring himself to call that pile of carnage "bodies" anymore.

When the lights came on in front of the glass, he rose slowly, leaned against the mirror for support, and followed the pathway as far from the scene of the crime as he could. He found the other end of the hall by accident.

Outside, it was still raining. Harsh, pelting drops attacked the earth and all life on it. There was a red glow to the clouds, the afterimage of sunset printed onto them. It would be night soon.

Christopher remembered Morgan's warning about being out at night. It seemed so long ago. That was back when he'd still trusted the sheriff. However, given what he had seen in town during the day, he reasoned that Morgan was probably right about nighttime being worse.

Now only needing to outrun time, Christopher found it was easier to maneuver through the amusement park, but not necessarily more pleasant. The decay was more prominent now. All the little details that Christopher hadn't noticed before stuck out like sore thumbs thanks to the better lighting and his own clarity.

The warped faces that appeared in the machinery, sneering, almost alive—as if they might attack at any moment (and with his luck, they might)—and the lonely, haunted feeling of the sheer emptiness of such large attractions truly touched him now. His own imagination struck hardest, wondering where else Prima and Terceira's macabre touches had affected the rides and operational sideshows.

His imagination was satisfied when he passed the carousel and saw that the usually fake horses were, in fact, very real, very dead, and very rotten. He could almost hear them neighing and stomping their hooves against the metal platform they were bolted to. Just as he was thinking how sad their situation was, one of them lifted its head, turned, and looked at him with empty eye sockets. It opened its mouth and whinnied, letting loose a dozen flies and spilling maggots onto the ground. The carousel music began to play louder and the ride creaked into motion, the rods lifting the heavy corpses up and down in time to the depraved, cheerful tune.

Christopher hobbled as best he could toward the now-visible exit of the amusement park. He passed through the rusty gates without a single moment of hesitation, making up his mind then and there to never look back and never return, even if Mickey begged him.

The more pressing issue was where he would spend the night. He could shack up in one of the abandoned houses on the way back to town, but that might lead to a run-in with Michael. After what he had seen, illusion or not, he wanted even less to do with that man. The police station was pretty much out, too, considering what Morgan had tried to do with him... though perhaps he was sober now. After all, Prima wasn't around to run the bar, and it was probably locked.

As if that would stop Morgan from getting alcohol if he was determined to satisfy his thirst.

Where does Matthew live? Christopher wondered. He was getting the idea that no one in the town was truly trustworthy—not even himself, apparently, though he would certainly consider himself to be better company than most—but out of everyone, surely he could rely on Matthew to offer him shelter for one night without attempting to murder him or do something equally as immoral.

But where did he live?

Not at the police station, that was for sure. Though, if that was where Morgan lived, then perhaps Matthew had also taken his place of work as his home. There must have been a back room in the deli, and if not, Christopher would settle for sleeping in a booth.

Christopher kept moving, exhausted from the day's events but determined to reach the town before nightfall. All the while, his mind fixated on one thought:

What did I do to deserve this?

CHAPTER NINE

The road seemed much shorter going back to town. Christopher didn't know whether that was a blessing or something he should remember and worry about later.

He passed the house in which he'd woken up, and noticed the number on it was indeed three-one-seven... which was strange, because the other house numbers were all around the six-hundreds, and Mary and Joseph's house had the same number. It occurred to Christopher that his latest ordeal, which had felt drawn out over years, had actually taken place within a few hours of his waking up in that house.

He hurried by the other houses, glancing their way only if he heard a noise or thought he saw something move. They were all boarded up, every window and door barred by planks of wood that had deep scratches in them. A few boards were broken, and the doors and windows they had protected swung back and forth in the wind, opening and closing, unwelcoming and forbidding. Those dwellings would offer him no protection from the monsters that ran loose in the town at night, and so he didn't stop to examine them as possible shelters.

Matthew's story about how everyone had tried to swim across the lake to the mainland and drowned no longer seemed likely, not when there were deep gouges scraped into the wood of the houses, shattered windows, and boards ripped from their places. Something had broken in and killed the people inside. Not something like the Jabberwock, but something with long, finger-like claws that could manipulate objects, with large, sharp teeth for crushing bone and tearing flesh. Something that was smart enough to understand the basic barricades and remove them.

The thought put new strength into Christopher's legs and he began to run again. His left leg protested any movement so he couldn't keep it up for more than a handful of yards, but whenever he felt brave enough to grit his teeth and bear it, he jogged along the road.

The rain fell harder and harder, until Christopher thought that he might as well try to swim through the air for all the good it would do. The rain was falling in such heavy sheets that he could hardly move, and that was saying nothing of the hurricane-force wind that made him stagger from one side of the road to the other. The cold seeped into his bones. He could barely breathe for all the water in the air, and if he didn't find shelter soon he might die. It would be a miracle if he didn't get hypothermia.

Christopher could hear the growling and moaning of monsters being flushed out of the rural neighborhoods toward the main road, and, even worse, the occasional honk of a clown nose. He shambled down the road as quickly as he could, a tired and broken shadow of a man hobbling through a water-logged wasteland. His greatest fear at the moment was not that he would be devoured by monsters or that he would be forced to take shelter with a rapist, but that he might slip in the mud. He knew he did not have the strength to get up again if he fell. It was only the thought that Mickey needed him—even if Christopher didn't understand how he could help the child—that kept him upright and moving forward.

After quite some time of fighting for every inch forward, Christopher spotted lights in the distance. They were not the pale fluorescent yellow of Godwin's Deli, but a loud orange-red. Under different circumstances Christopher would have avoided them, but he didn't have the luxury of being picky.

He warily veered toward the lights. There was no telling who or what might be inside the building or how they would receive him, but anything was better than freezing to death in the downpour. As he drew nearer, he could discern lettering on the sign over the door: "Garden of Eden Nursery and Gift Shoppe." It must have been Abel's business, lights left on and waiting for an owner that would never return.

Christopher thought it was the least he could do to see that the electricity was shut off and the store locked up. Surely Abel's soul—wherever it was—wouldn't mind if he sheltered there for the night. After all, he'd been *tricked* into eating

Don't think about it.

The door was unlocked, as he had expected, and a bell jingled when Christopher stepped inside. He flashed it an irritated frown. Did every door in this town have an inappropriately cheerful bell?

To his left was the register, and in front of him were rows of shelves cluttered with things like postcards, coffee mugs, and candy. Above him was a sign pointing right that read, "Nursery this way; watch your step!"

It was unsettling to see such a normal setting amidst the paranormal bloodshed that Christopher had been witness to that day, let alone since he'd woken up in the hospital. All that was missing was elevator music and a few tourists looking for souvenirs and gifts. Christopher found himself flipping absentmindedly through the postcards, which were all flower-themed and bore the store's logo.

The water dripping down Christopher's hands began to feel thicker, and as he turned through the cards the flowers began to look sickly, browning and losing petals rapidly.

The last card he came to was entirely black—until a wide, bloodshot eye opened in its center.

Christopher jumped and dropped the cards, all of which now bore the staring eye. They regarded him for a moment, then turned to look toward the nursery. A scratchy hissing reached his ears. "Lost... missing... never going home, never seen again..."

He clapped his hands over his ears and stomped his foot down on one of the postcards, causing a small spurt of blood to color the floor.

"Stop it!"

The eyes disappeared and were replaced once more by images of colorful flowers, except for the crushed daisy beneath Christopher's foot.

"I'm going insane," Christopher whimpered with his head in his hands. He stood there like that for a moment, struggling to catch his breath and hang on to what little bit of reality he could reach.

He looked for a weapon. Abel might be dead, and Prima and Terceira too, but that didn't mean he was safe. Everyone in the town, save for maybe Mickey and himself, had skeletons in their closets, and not the type that were inclined to stay dead. He was sure some new enemy would appear at any moment.

The store was well-equipped with souvenir switchblades and Swiss army knives, but they weren't adequate weapons. Christopher would have to be close to his target— closer than he'd want to be— to use them. He might as well still have the scalpel he'd found in the hospital. He needed something with a handle, something that could attack from a short distance, if not more. He didn't expect Abel to have a gun, but a hatchet, maybe, would suffice.

He searched the gift shop for a while longer but didn't find anything useful, so he took one of the switchblades and flicked the blade out, just in case, as he made his way to the nursery.

Not surprisingly, the nursery was much larger than the gift shop, sprawling out from the doorway almost endlessly. To the right were things like potted flowers, rose bushes, and other such decorative plants to keep inside or outside. To the left were more agricultural flora, like vegetables and fruit trees. Against the walls were multiple types of pesticides, mulches, herbicides, and anything else a gardener would ever need.

It didn't much matter, though, since all the plants were dead and withered. The only things "growing" in the store were the decaying hands that reached up out of the flower pots.

How long has Abel been dead? Christopher wondered as he walked through the rows of dried plants and rotting limbs. He reached out to touch a leaf, and it crumbled under the gentle pressure. The whole plant then disintegrated into nothing but a pile of crushed leaves and stalks. He instinctively looked to check if anyone had seen him destroy the plant so he could apologize, but of course no one was there. He breathed a sigh that was less relief and more than a little sad.

He had found somewhere safe to stay the night, that was the important thing. He could make his way to the delicatessen in the morning and then begin his search for Mickey again. He doubted he would ever be truly reunited with the child, but if he managed to catch another fleeting glimpse of the boy, maybe Mickey might offer some clue as to where Christopher could go next, or what had happened in the town, or why he was there in the first place.

Christopher started to walk again, only to trip and fall to his hands and knees. He looked to see what had tripped him and saw he had somehow gotten his foot entangled in a plant root. He pulled himself free and stood, took another step, and felt something tighten around his ankle—another root.

Christopher glanced around the room and spotted a hatchet off to one corner. He tugged his foot free of the root and lunged for the weapon. He folded the knife and put it in his pocket before grabbing the small ax.

The roots continued to creep toward him, and he chopped into them as they did. The hatchet had been sharpened recently and, much to his relief, it cut cleanly. He had worried that it might stick in the wood, and after too many chops it might, but for the time being it was a reliable weapon.

Christopher forced his fear away as more roots snaked toward him, converging from the ground, walls, and ceiling. He stepped over them as fast as possible, not daring to let his feet get caught, and picked his way back to the front of the gift shop only to find that the roots had already predicted his movement. They'd grown over the door too thickly for him to cut them away. If he wanted out, he would have to kill them at their source.

He raced over the vines and back into the nursery, ready to slice to pieces whatever was causing the roots to grow, tracing them back to whatever monstrous plant they were growing from.

He did not expect it to have teeth.

At the furthest point in the nursery, growing out of a comically small flower pot, was a massive mouth. As far as Christopher could tell it had no eyes, ears, or nose—only a gaping maw, rimmed with two sets of teeth that were sharply pointed, each glistening fang as long as his arm. The mouth itself filled the expanse between the table on which the pot sat and the ceiling, making it easily taller than Christopher. It would likely swallow him whole if he strayed too close to the mouth.

Just when Christopher was thinking he might try to make a run for the overgrown front door after all, the roots sealed the door between the nursery and gift shop. They covered everything: the walls, the floor, the ceiling, everywhere but the lights that the giant plant needed to survive. He gripped the hatchet tightly and braced himself.

The mouth leaned forward, though not far. Christopher managed to jump out of the way, but he tripped over one of the roots upon his landing. The root then wrapped around his body and lifted him, drawing him closer to the monster.

He raised the hatchet and chopped frantically at the root until it dropped him a few inches from the teeth, which had begun to close in anticipation of a meal. Christopher landed on his feet and darted to the side of the plant monster, trying to get out of range of its jaws. He swung the ax into the base of the maw, where its stem extended from the soil. He succeeded in striking his mark, but failed to sever it entirely. His weapon barely made a dent in the strong stem, not that anyone would know it the way the plant shrieked.

The roots swirled around him, wrapping around his legs and midsection. They tried to grab Christopher's arms as well, but he moved them too quickly, sinking the hatchet deep into the stem with every ounce of strength he could muster. The roots tried to drag him back, but thankfully the hatchet stuck fast in the core of the plant, and he held it tightly.

The monster cried out again and Christopher echoed it. The roots that had wrapped around his waist were constricting and pulling; he felt as if they might tear him in two, given the way they were pulling on his legs and now his arms. Perhaps the plant was trying to do just that, breaking him into bite-sized pieces.

If Christopher's leg hadn't been broken before, it most certainly was now.

The hatchet remained lodged in the main stem, and Christopher clung to it. The plant jerked him backwards again. The blade came free as he was thrown to the front of the nursery and sliced straight through the plant itself, severing the stem to just an inch. The momentum tipped the mouth to its side and the weight of it snapped the last bit of trunk that remained. Bright green sap oozed from the wound.

Christopher coughed, trying to pull breath back into his lungs. He wriggled free of the limp roots and lifted his sweater to see how much damage had been done to his mid-section. Ugly reddish-purple welts were already rising around his stomach and back, and he wouldn't be surprised to see them on his legs and arms as well.

There was a cracking noise, and he instinctively covered his head with his arms as the roots began to fall from the ceiling and walls into great piles of kindling, freeing up the doorways. When he dragged himself back into the gift shop and looked out of the windows, he saw that the rain had stopped, but it was still night. Shapes moved about in the darkness, and Christopher was not inclined to chance an encounter with any of them. He limped to the door and made sure it was locked. On top of that, he shoved one of the display shelves in front of the entrance to barricade it.

He picked up a lighter from the counter, returned to the nursery, and grabbed a pile of roots. He brought them back to the gift shop and started a small fire that he could keep contained with his still sopping wet clothing. He replaced his sweater with a t-shirt off the rack that had a picture of a blue rose and read "Garden of Eden Nursery and Gift Shoppe, Wonderland, OR: Where dreams become reality."

The fire crackled to life and Christopher felt a little bit of warmth find its way back into his numb body. He looked around the store again. The roots hadn't damaged the walls or ceiling. In fact, aside from his little pile of firewood, he didn't see any signs of the tendrils at all. Those in the pile looked more like some of the window boards he'd seen outside than a natural root.

Christopher no longer cared if he imagined it or not.

Although he relished the break from running or fighting for his life, just sitting on the floor and staring at the fire got boring fast. He started talking to himself to pass the time.

There are many different ways to talk to oneself. For instance, if he had said out loud, "Good job, Christopher," for successfully getting himself out of a dangerous situation, that would have been just fine. Or if he had muttered some kind of plan regarding what to do next, that would have been fine, too. But Christopher was not doing these things, and he was not so much talking to himself as having a full-blown conversation even though nobody else was present.

"Nasty weather lately, don't you think? Oh, yeah, well, it's an island and it's fall now, what are you going to do? You ought to come in the summertime when the weather's nice. Well, I don't think I'll be doing that, thanks, I have a job, you know, with the children and such. You work with children? Oh, yes, it's a lot of fun, really! I wish we had the money to get them costumes on Halloween though, that would be a real treat for them, but there are too many to take trick-or-treating. Have you got a favorite? We aren't supposed to, but yes, Mickey. Cutest little kid, but I worry about him sometimes. He's out here alone by himself, and I've been trying to find him because he needs food and care and I don't know if he's been getting either one. The people in this town are strange, too. No offense. None taken. Where have you looked so far? Uh, the school and the amusement park. I figured a child might go there. I might have tried the bookstore, too, Mickey loves books, but it was boarded up... a little odd, really. What? It was boarded up from the inside and most of the buildings are boarded up from the outside. Maybe I should try it when I go back. I suppose you could."

Christopher stayed awake all night long acting out conversations with the shadows on the walls. Only when he was certain he hadn't seen a shape outside in the dark (for it was still very cloudy) for at least an hour did he venture to guess that it was finally morning. He grabbed the hatchet and opened the front door, remembering just before he left to turn the lights off and lock up the shop so no one would break in.

His next move was to head to the deli, which was thankfully not far away. It was still early, but if his theory about Matthew living there was correct, then it ought to be alright to knock and see if he could be let in.

Despite how close the deli was, it took Christopher a while to reach it. He was sore from the encounter with the Jabberwock, injuring his leg multiple times (though it was, miraculously, starting to feel better already), and the fight with the plant monster. He desperately wished the hospital was operational, but given what he had found there, perhaps it was better that it wasn't.

The lights were out at the bar. They wouldn't be turned on ever again.

Christopher's stomach churned and he leaned against the side of the building. Even if they had been cannibals, even if they had been about to kill him, Prima and Terceira hadn't deserved their torturous demise. He had managed to avoid thinking about it through the night, but now that he was out and about the town again all the weight of the previous days' events came crashing back down onto his already fractured mind.

Don't think about it, he urged himself. *Just forget it, get to the deli, and plan your next move. Things aren't so bad. You'll see. It's so much nicer to forget about these unpleasant things.*

Of course, he had to plan what he was going to say when he got there. Even if Matthew might not be as bad as Morgan, the fact that the two were related would probably cause the delicatessen's allegiance to be swayed toward the officer's side. But Christopher didn't need a place to stay; he just needed a place to compose himself and maybe unearth some more clues.

As far as Christopher could gather from his memories of the dinner party, the madness was Michael's fault... but considering that Prima and Terceira weren't exactly in their right minds either, who could say? They might have been lying to make him mistrust Michael... not that he'd needed any help on that front.

He'd have to ask Matthew about it. The deli owner would hopefully have some idea why Michael might be blamed for the island's problems. Whether Michael actually had anything to do with the madness didn't matter, because people's suspicions—even when wrong and proven so—could influence their behaviors and actions. Besides, the vagrant obviously wasn't even close to being human, judging by the way he had shown up out of nowhere when Christopher had been in trouble and

I said don't think about it!

Plan in mind, Christopher tried to pay more attention to the walk. Besides, it would be rude not to say hello to all the nice, faceless townsfolk who had emerged from their houses. It wasn't a particularly nice day, but after the storm, even the overcast weather was a huge improvement. If the nicer weather hadn't brought them out, the need to clear fallen tree branches from the roads certainly had.

They turned to look at Christopher as he passed, and he waved to them out of politeness. The ones who had arms waved back whether they had faces or not. A couple of children ran past him, heading toward the school; it must be a weekday after all. One of them lagged behind, adjusting his thick-rimmed glasses and breathing hard. The name tag sewn lovingly onto his backpack read, "Stanley."

The lights in Godwin's Deli were on and the door wasn't locked. The specials on the sign outside had changed, too, so Matthew had to be there.

Christopher let himself in and was immediately greeted by Cheshire's meowing. The cat bounded toward him and rubbed against his legs.

Matthew's voice came from the back room. "Morgan, it's too early and I don't want to talk to you right now."

"It's Christopher."

"Oh, Chris, hi!" Matthew came to the front of the shop, stopping behind the counter when he saw the orderly. "Oh my God, you look *terrible*. What happened to you?"

"A lot of things. I don't think I have time to tell you about it right now. I have to stay focused. Can I just get some food or... actually, never mind, I don't want any food from you."

Matthew glanced out of the windows before responding. "Uh... uh-huh. But this is a sandwich shop. There's not really a lot I can do for you if you aren't here to eat a sandwich. At least let me give you some water. You look like you really need it."

He grabbed a plastic cup and filled it with water from the fountain machine, then set it on the counter to coax Christopher out of the doorway. Christopher stared at the cup for a minute. What if Matthew had put poison in the reservoir? There were a number of poisons that could blend in seamlessly with water. And Christopher was more than wary of accepting food or drink from anyone on the island.

Matthew sighed and took a generous sip. "See? It's fine. And it's not tap water."

Christopher approached the counter and snatched the cup, spilling a fair bit of the liquid as he gulped it down. He did feel a little bit better after drinking it, and Matthew refilled the cup as soon as he was done. After the third serving, Christopher was much calmer and a lot less dizzy, but Matthew still needed to help him find a seat before he collapsed.

The two sat in a booth together. Christopher slumped over the table, lack of rest steadily catching up to him, though he couldn't lower his guard enough to actually fall asleep.

"Did..." Matthew took a breath. "Did my brother do something to you?"

Christopher shifted so his back was to Matthew. He really didn't want to go into this now.

"I thought so. I'm actually kind of surprised you came back. The way he was carrying on, I thought maybe he'd killed you," Matthew went on. "Haven't seen him that emotional in a while. He wouldn't say what he did, but he just kept crying. I'm guessing that part was mostly the alcohol."

"Can we not talk about it?" Christopher asked. "I have other things I want to ask you."

Matthew kept right on talking about it. "I know my brother isn't that great of a guy, but I figured he must have really crossed a line with you, which is why I thought maybe he killed you or something. But here you are, so I guess it wasn't that. And I don't suppose you're going to tell me what he did. He's been in a funk ever since, and it's getting really irritating, which is why I was snappish when you came in. It is just too *early* to deal with his emotional baggage."

Christopher dropped his head onto the table repeatedly. *Forget, forget, forget...*

"So, are you alright?"

He tilted his head to look up at Matthew. "Yeah. I'm super."

"Okay. Water usually helps me; glad it worked for you, too. Hang on a second." Matthew stood and hurried to the back room again, then returned with a blanket. "I'm not using this right now, anyway." He put it over Christopher's shoulders. "You were looking a little shaken up. Try to take deep breaths and focus on one thing at a time."

"I'm trying to focus on finding Mickey. Please tell me you've seen him, or have some idea about where he might be."

"You know, I have problems with Morgan, too."

Christopher sighed. Was Matthew *ever* going to drop this subject?

"So, whatever he did, please don't judge me based on it," Matthew continued. "We're really nothing alike. I probably relate more to you than to him."

Christopher glanced up at Matthew. He was smiling in a reassuring way, but his eyes had a faraway, glassy look in them, like he was thinking hard about something else. Christopher doubted Morgan had treated them the same way, but it did make him a little more comfortable to know that Matthew wasn't likely to side with his twin on the issue. He had somewhere safer to stay, after all.

"Morgan will probably show up soon," Matthew said. "If you'd like, you can take a nap in the back. He won't go in there, and if he asks I'll just tell him I haven't seen you."

Nodding, Christopher let Matthew help him out of the booth and to the back of the deli. The room was a little chilly since the window had been cracked open, and it reminded Christopher of his room back at the asylum. Unlike Morgan's office, this room was clean and organized; he assumed that the odd smell was a byproduct of the deli's wares, maybe some old ingredients that had started to turn. At least the mattress was soft.

Matthew left the room and closed the door. Christopher lay there, still alert for any sign that Matthew might turn out to be a psychotic killer, but several minutes passed and he didn't hear anything on the other side of the door that was in any way suspicious. He tried the door, just to be sure, and found that it opened with ease; he wasn't locked in.

His fatigue was giving him no choice at this point but to trust the brown-eyed twin. Christopher returned to the mattress and let himself fall asleep for a while. He could question Matthew about the town's oddities after he'd had time to recover.

*I*t was starting to get dark again when Christopher woke up. He had only meant to take a brief nap, but his body had demanded otherwise and he'd slept through the entire day. Frustrated with himself but feeling much better, he rolled onto his back and stared up at the glow-in-the-dark planet stickers on the ceiling of Matthew's room.

What was he going to do? He had to choose the questions he asked carefully. Saying the wrong thing might cause Matthew to withdraw, like mention of the hospital had done to Michael.

Think, he urged himself. *What do you know? What information do you have to go on?*

Prima and Terceira were no longer a threat to his miserable existence, and neither was Abel's giant plant monster. Even if he was remorseful about how they had died, and that they'd had to die in the first place, the fact that they could no longer kill and eat him did provide some guilty comfort.

He couldn't find Mickey, nor did he expect to, if Mickey was even anywhere to be found. It wouldn't be too far-fetched to say that all of the boy's appearances had been in his mind. Mickey might show up again to help, or he might not; either way, Christopher wasn't going to depend on his advice or guidance. Besides, he was supposed to be the one rescuing Mickey, not the other way around.

Morgan was a rapist, and that was bad enough for Christopher to go out of his way to avoid him. Maybe he was being too harsh, maybe he should give the officer a chance to redeem himself or at least apologize, but Christopher didn't really care or think the man deserved it. From their brief conversation earlier, he gathered Matthew felt much the same way. And if *Matthew* wouldn't forgive his brother, why should Christopher?

Michael was insane at best, inhuman at worst, so Christopher was better off avoiding him, too.

The same went for Joseph and Mary. In retrospect, they were probably the most harmless residents of the town. They hadn't done anything wrong, per se, they were just creepy. However, Christopher was certain that if he returned to their home, he would discover their innocent doll collection was anything but. Then he'd have to fend off hundreds of rabid dolls with nothing but his hatchet, and he was not keen to do that.

The bridge wasn't ever going to be fixed, so it would be useless to investigate the other end of the island. There were probably monsters in the water, too, so it wasn't like he could try to swim to the mainland. He wasn't even a strong swimmer.

Everywhere he went, something—supernatural or not—attacked him. He was sure that if he stayed still long enough, something would come and find him. There was no escape, no waiting out the madness. The real question was whether it was better to find or be found.

The map was completely ruined and he had lost his flashlight. All he had left was useless information, a hatchet, a pocket knife, and a facetious t-shirt. And the hatchet's blade had probably been dulled considerably by the battle with the plant monster. It would be difficult to use in combat again.

Pretty pathetic, he thought harshly. *I know I'm missing something important, some tiny, important detail that will solve everything. If only I could figure out what questions to ask.*

He stretched and winced; he was still badly hurt and in need of medical care, but that would have to wait. He was almost out of bed when there was a commotion in the deli and Cheshire darted into the room, a black and white streak leaping onto the bed. His hackles were raised and his tail was puffed out. Claws dug into Christopher's leg as the cat scrambled to curl up in a wrinkle on the blanket.

Christopher hoped Matthew had just dropped something and startled the cat, but he already knew that wasn't going to be the case. He grabbed the hatchet, opened the door all the way, and reentered the deli to see Morgan helping Matthew into a booth. Maybe he'd fallen and injured himself? The officer took a seat next to him and dropped his head into his hands.

Please don't let him be drunk, Christopher prayed, and cleared his throat to get their attention.

Morgan looked up first. "Hey... hey, Chris. What are you doing here?"

"I came to talk to Matthew," Christopher answered sharply. "I was hoping to be gone before you got here, but I fell asleep for longer than I meant, and now here we are."

"You can't talk to him right now," Morgan said. "What did you want to talk to him about? I might be able to help."

"Why can't I talk to him? He's right there."

"I'm sorry, but you can't talk to Matthew. And I'm sorry about what happened at the school. Really! I would never have done something like that, even if I was drunk. I have no idea what came over me—it was like my body was moving on its own."

"I can't really say that I care," Christopher snapped. "No matter *what* your excuse is, nothing could ever make me forgive what you tried to do. Do you honestly think 'sorry' is enough? It doesn't work that way."

"I didn't expect you to forgive me. I don't deserve forgiveness. I just want you to know that I'm sorry."

Morgan took his gun out of its holster, and Christopher took a step back. He made a pitiful attempt to defend himself by holding the hatchet between him and Morgan. "What are you doing?"

"Like I said... I don't deserve to be forgiven. I don't deserve to live," Morgan answered. Christopher could see now that his eyes were red and bloodshot from crying, not alcohol. He started to sob.

Throughout all of this, Matthew hadn't said or done anything, or even looked up from the table.

"Morgan? Morgan... what's wrong with Matthew?" Christopher asked.

"I told you, you can't talk to him," Morgan cried. "I had to do it. Had to!"

"Had to do what? *What did you do to Matthew*?"

Morgan let out a wail and dropped his head into his hands again. "Mattie! I'm so sorry!"

"What did you do, Morgan?" Christopher growled and pushed past him, ignoring the gun and giving Matthew a rough shake. His head lolled to the side without any resistance and now that Christopher was closer to him he could see that his eyes were glazed over and his skin was growing pale at an alarming rate. He was cold. Christopher couldn't feel a pulse or see the rise and fall in his chest that would have signified breathing.

"Why would you do that? Why would you kill your own brother?" he demanded. "Matthew didn't do anything wrong!"

"What do you know?!" Morgan shouted, rising to his feet and pointing the gun at Christopher with a trembling hand. The steel felt frigid against his chest and he stumbled back, the hatchet forgotten in his hand. "What do you know about anything? Just because you took some psychology class in college or whatever, you think you can judge what the rest of us do? Who gave you the right to stand on your damned pedestal? You don't know anything about Mattie, you don't know anything about me, you don't know *anything*!"

Christopher inhaled and exhaled deeply. He was getting frustrated and reckless.

If Morgan wasn't so obviously in need of a shoulder to cry on, Christopher had no doubt he would have already be dead. This was a man who had just killed his own brother in cold blood, for Christ's sake; there was no telling what he might do next.

"So, enlighten me. Tell me about Matthew. What did he do? Why did you want to kill him?"

"I didn't want to!" Morgan cried. "I didn't. I love Mattie. I only wanted to see him smile. That's why I did everything. Everything. From the time we were kids, everything I've ever done was to make Mattie happy. I was going to protect him from all the bad guys.

"The people at the orphanage never noticed him a whole lot, you see. I was loud, so they gave me a little attention, but Mattie was always quiet. They'd forget to feed him, or just wouldn't care enough to. So I had to get food for him. I had to raise him. And I did a good job! We were adopted later by some pretty nice guys, changed our last names to Godwin and everything, but I never stopped watching out for him. Even when we got sent to the hospital I made sure he was safe."

"Then why kill him now?" Christopher asked.

"I told you. Everything I've ever done has been to make Mattie happy. He... Mattie knew things. Things he couldn't have possibly known. Like the day there was that fire at school, he knew it was going to happen. And the hospital. He was always terrified of that place, said the doctors were doing things they shouldn't be doing to people." Morgan shook his head. "He saw things, he had horrible nightmares, but he always kept it under control. It was when the bridge burned down that things changed."

So Matthew *could* have provided more information. And now it was lost, unless Christopher could coax something out of Morgan.

"Changed? How so?"

"Mattie just *changed*. I remember when I got up that morning, he was in the bathroom, holding a razor. Looking at it. And I remember thinking, 'Oh my God, he's going to kill himself!' And when I asked him why, he told me... he told me..."

"What did he tell you?"

"He said, 'But Morgan, we're already dead!' Really calmly, too. I told him he was crazy—how could we be dead when we were walking around in our house and things were just like they always were? Yeah, maybe our dads weren't there 'cause they went with some of the others to check out the bridge and see if there was a way across to get help, but things were still normal then. But he was absolutely certain, and he told me things were going to get a whole lot worse, and that we should just try. He wanted to know if we could die again, I guess, and escape like that."

Christopher almost asked if it worked, but that nonsensical question answered itself as soon as he'd thought it. Instead, he let Morgan continue uninterrupted.

"I wouldn't let him do that. I did everything I could do to stop him, to get him to stop trying. I couldn't be there all the time, though! So I..." Morgan sobbed for a few moments, unable to get the words out. "So I broke into the hospital. There was a secret entrance to the first floor where the pharmacy was, that no one else ever found after it burned down. A broken window... you can only find it by going through the graveyard. We weren't supposed to go there, it was too dangerous, but I went in, and I found the pharmacy, and I stole some drugs that hadn't burned... not a single flake of ash on them... like they were waiting just for me."

"What drugs?"

"Valium, Vicodin, stuff like that. Strong painkillers. I slipped them into Mattie's food." Morgan let out another series of sobs that rocked his entire body. "What kind of person does that? I drugged my own brother! I remember the first time I did it. I was just so scared of losing him, especially after everyone else started disappearing. I was willing to do anything to keep him alive. And I almost did lose him that first time. I gave him too much. But that didn't stop me. I had to make sure he didn't try to kill himself, even if that meant making it so he couldn't get out of bed without my help."

Christopher shuddered. He'd been sleeping in Matthew's bed mere minutes ago. It was creepy enough that he'd slept in a dead man's bed, but how many times had Matthew been confined to it against his will?

"It scared him. He didn't know why it was happening, so of course he was scared, and with everyone else gone, he thought he was going to be next. I don't think he ever really *wanted* to die, or whatever he was attempting to do, he just thought he had to. I had to fess up and tell him... but by that time, he was addicted to the pills, and it was my fault. I did that to him. And it didn't fix things. He still knew, still insisted we were dead, he just lost the ability to do anything about it."

"Did he ever tell you why he thought you were dead?"

"He never explained it. He just said that we were, that it was a thought he had and couldn't let go of. Like I said, Mattie always just *knew* things. And you know, I think I believe him now. The monsters, the fact that there's no one else in this town, that there's no way to get onto this island and yet somehow the deli never runs out of food and the hospital never ran out of pills, and suddenly you appear out of no-freakin'-where..." Again he paused to collect himself. "Not just that, but over time, when I went to go get Mattie's drugs, do you know what happened? There were stronger drugs waiting for me, for when Mattie built up a strong enough tolerance to whatever I had him on that it didn't keep him sedated. Oxycodone, methadone, heroin, morphine, whatever I needed! And the more I thought about that, the more I thought that this is what Hell must be like. I'm sure of it."

Morgan studied the gun. "And that got me thinking that Mattie had the right idea after all. Ending it, before he could go insane. He saw it coming. He knew what we'd all become if we spent enough time in this place. So I... I finally decided to let him die. And you know what was waiting for me at the hospital this morning? A syringe full of fucking sodium thiopental to do the job! He didn't even fight... he didn't even fight..."

Morgan put the gun to his temple. "I don't deserve a pretty death like that. Chris, you go to the hospital and finish what you started there. Maybe you don't have to be trapped like the rest of us. You're a good man, and I'm sorry for what happened."

He smiled. His finger was steadier now.

"No, wait! Prima said this was my fault, that I brought monsters here or something like that and that's how this all started. She was prepared to kill me for it. You have to tell me what this place was like before I came here, or how it's changed—*something*! If you're really sorry, then help me!"

Morgan just smiled at him sadly and pulled the trigger without another word. Blood and brains splattered across the table as Morgan's body toppled back into the seat, smearing gore over Matthew's body.

Christopher stared for a minute.

It occurred to him that some of the blood had splashed onto him, as well.

His lower lip trembled, and the corners of his mouth pulled themselves into a grin as he laughed. He just laughed and laughed until there were tears streaming down his face, washing the blood off of his cheeks.

Cheshire stood at the door, mewing. The former orderly leaned down and picked up the cat. Cheshire purred while Christopher rubbed the base of his ears.

"It's just you and me left," Christopher said. "Just you and me, we're the only sane people left on this island. But I'm going to get the answers. If it's the last thing I do, I'm going to find out what all of this is."

Christopher locked the door and turned off the lights. He settled into the booth furthest away from the twins' corpses, still holding Cheshire. He sat there in silence for a long time, thinking. Bethlem Royal Medical Center was the only place left to go—and the last place that he wanted to go, at that. He had no idea what he would find there, but he was sure that it wasn't going to be a picnic.

The minutes stretched into hours. It was definitely night now, and despite having spent most of the day in bed he was starting to feel tired again, but he couldn't sleep for fear that the bodies would come alive and attack him. Cheshire stayed awake beside him, purring in his ear like a lullaby. He would need his strength and whatever sanity he could salvage for what was to come.

After what felt like a lethargic eternity, Christopher left the booth and, shuddering, shuffled over to Morgan's body.

It hadn't moved an inch. The blood had already begun to turn a charred black color as it dried. He took the gun and checked it. There were still bullets inside, and he took the holster off of Morgan's corpse to carry the weapon.

Cheshire meowed.

"Yeah," Christopher said. "I think it's time that this ended, too."

He walked out of the deli, heading straight for the graveyard.

It was drizzling outside, not that Christopher had expected nice weather.

It was strange. All the way to the graveyard, the only noise he had heard was the water falling to the earth. No shrieks. No screams. No wails. No scraping sounds.

Just the rain.

As he approached the graveyard, situated conveniently at the top of a large hill, he turned and surveyed the town. It was eerie, knowing with absolute certainty that there was no human life left there. Everyone there was dead, except for maybe Joseph and Mary, though Christopher had his suspicions that they weren't human at all.

The only way out of the town was through death. Christopher thought back to how close he had come to killing himself at the hospital. If he had known then what he knew now, he imagined he probably would have gone through with it. He probably would have killed Mickey, too, to spare him from the same horrors.

How would he have done it? It would have had to be painless. He wouldn't have wanted Mickey to suffer. Maybe he'd have used pills or a lethal injection, like Morgan had done.

A light smile graced Christopher's lips. They may have died in completely horrible ways, but at least they were all free. It was a relieving thought. They weren't suffering anymore.

The worst that can happen to me is death, he thought. *So really... there's nothing to worry about. No matter what happens, I'll escape. One way or another, the pain and fear will end.*

Of course, he would prefer not to die. He had to protect Mickey, didn't he? Had to rescue Mickey, too, even if 'rescue' meant 'kill.' He would do anything, whatever it took, to make sure that Mickey didn't end up like the townspeople... like himself... raving mad, eternally tortured by monsters, both real and hallucinated. Always cold. Christopher put a hand to his forehead and discovered that he was feverish, burning up and probably at risk of death—how he was even still standing and walking was a mystery. He shouldn't have been able to get up if he was that sick.

It didn't matter.

First he had to reach the hospital, get to the second floor, to room three-seventeen. All he had to do to accomplish that was figure out where Morgan's secret entrance was and find a way up to the second floor. He didn't like the idea of having to crawl through that tunnel again, with all those spiders and other creepy-crawlies.

There was a way into the first floor somewhere. Christopher was beginning to believe that if it hadn't been important, Morgan wouldn't have been allowed to tell him about it. The puppet master that controlled the town had permitted it.

Standing there, he began to feel sad. The shock of Morgan and Matthew's deaths was finally sinking in. Yes, they were free, but he missed them, more than he thought was possible, and he would have given anything to have them with him as he descended into the final level of this Hell. Matthew's knowledge, Morgan's aggression and weaponry—both would have been useful and uplifting. After all, Christopher had never fired a gun in his life, and though it seemed fairly self-explanatory he was sure that Morgan would have had much better aim under stress and a much better knowledge of where to shoot which monsters.

They hadn't deserved what had happened to them. As far as Christopher could see, they'd had no control over it. They were merely pawns in the town's psychotic design, a source of entertainment for an unknown malevolent force that they had been helpless to stand against. Maybe Christopoher should have forgiven Morgan after all. What if he truly hadn't been acting according to his own will?

How long had Morgan felt it necessary to keep his brother drugged to keep him alive? How long had Matthew wanted nothing more than to slip away into the eternal dream? How long had they both been suffering, with no way of knowing when or if it would ever end, save for death?

They're free now. They're together, and happy, Christopher thought in an attempt to save himself from the sorrow and guilt that he faced whenever anyone or thing died. It was for the best that they were dead, and that he would probably be joining them soon.

He turned from the town square and made his way up the rest of the hill, his thighs soon sore from pushing against the slippery ground. The trail to the graveyard was well-worn, probably by all the parents of children who had died in the school fire, and the families of the patients who had died in the hospital fire. There would have been no graves for those who had simply vanished, victims of Prima and Terceira's cannibalism or the jaws of other monsters.

It was, of course, silent as he moved. Unnaturally silent. Not even the sound of Christopher's shoes made noise when they touched the ground or rustled stalks of grass that had grown over the winding pathway. He stayed alert, ears straining for any noise that might signal a monster nearby, any noise he was making that would give his position away.

There was nothing; he kept moving and tried to think happy thoughts.

"Read this one!"

"Alright, alright. The point of this is so that you go to sleep, you know. It's pointless if you're so excited that you're awake for another hour!"

"I know, but I can't help it. It's my favorite."

"Of course. Okay, are you all tucked in?"

"Yes!"

"And you're going to listen quietly and not interject at every other page?"

The boy nodded, then shook his head enthusiastically. Christopher smiled and began to read the poem that started the book:

> *"Child of the pure unclouded brow*
> *And dreaming eyes of wonder!*
> *Though time be fleet, and I and thou*
> *Are half a life asunder,*
> *Thy loving smile will surely hail*
> *The love-gift of a fairy-tale.*
> *I have not seen thy sunny face,*
> *Nor heard thy silver laughter:*
> *No thought of me shall find a place*
> *In thy young life's hereafter—*
> *Enough that now thou wilt not fail*
> *To listen to my fairy-tale..."*

*Christopher finished the poem and intended to continue
to chapter one, but he saw that Mickey was already fast asleep.
He closed the book, smoothed the boy's hair, and left the room.
"Good night, Mickey," he said. "Chapter one next time."*

The graveyard was, appropriately, devoid of all life.

All life. No trees. No grass, even. The greenery ended abruptly at the edge of the graveyard, not extending a single blade past the gate.

Rows and rows of headstones stuck out of murky, brown earth—damp sludge that sucked Christopher's legs, as if trying to bring him into a grave of his own sooner than he was ready for it. It occurred to him that the tunnel would be flooded and possibly caved in.

As he approached hospital, his eyes scanned the lettering on the headstones in his wake.

*Primrose "Prima" McClatchey
October 29, 1936 – December 18, 1980
A woman whose hair was as red as the blood of her victims*

*Terceira Esperanza Garcia
March 2, 1936 – December 18, 1980
Beauty is only skin deep*

Christopher squinted at the engravings. The dates had to be wrong. It was still October of 1970, last he'd checked.

He kept going and spotted a larger headstone with two names on it. The grave had been freshly dug, and the smell of peat reached his nose.

*Morgan William Godwin and Matthew Jeffrey Godwin
April 10, 1950 – June 2, 1978
Devoted in life, devoted in death*

Christopher shook his head. If Morgan and Matthew had died after Prima and Terceira, then why was their death date two years prior? His head was starting to hurt trying to decipher these nonsensical graves, graves that had probably only been placed there to make him question reality even more than he already was.

Still, he couldn't look away from the next grave he saw.

Christopher Anthony Robinson
September 2, 1948 – October 20, 1970
A liar

He kicked the headstone. "I am *not* a liar!"

Lightning split the sky and the rain began to fall harder.

Christopher hurried toward the hospital at a faster pace, looking it over for the secret entrance and wishing that Morgan had given better directions. His foot hit something, and he tripped but did not fall. When he looked over his shoulder to see what he had stumbled on, he saw one last grave.

"Mickey" Walters
May 20, 1959 – July 31, 1984
Keep smiling!

Now that was going too far, but the epitaph was something Christopher needed. He knelt and hugged the tombstone. He wasn't the least bit surprised when the cold stone turned to the soft hair, skin, and wool that he was more accommodated to holding this close.

"This is it, huh? The final stretch?" he murmured.

Mickey gave him a small squeeze before shifting out of the hug, leading the way to the secret entrance of the hospital. It would have taken a while to check the windows on the side of the hospital facing the graveyard to find the right one. It was boarded up, but if Christopher jiggled the lowest board just right, he was able to push it far enough to nudge his way in.

The first floor of the hospital looked exactly as expected. It was cold, and the fluorescent lighting did nothing to help that. It was a lot bigger than the other floors had been, though to be fair, Christopher had been pretty limited in his movements down the hallways. Since the first floor didn't have any closed rooms, he was free to explore it in its entirety.

Off to one side there was a pharmacy, and on the counter sat cloth bandages and peroxide. There was even a bag in which to carry them. Christopher checked himself again; he didn't have any cuts that needed attention, but he took the bag and the items all the same.

He opened a few of the cabinets. There was a bag of crackers in one, and a can of soup. He ate a few crackers before continuing; it didn't do much to sate his hunger, but he felt a little better after getting *something* into his stomach.

Christopher could feel Mickey watching him from the staircase that led to the second floor. He was taking too much time, and he knew that trying to delay the inevitable was pointless, but that wouldn't stop him. He stowed the rest of the crackers in the bag and, after searching the first floor for any other useful items, joined the boy at the stairs. He gave Mickey's hair one last affectionate ruffle before beginning his ascent.

He knew that when he looked back, the boy would be gone.

CHAPTER ELEVEN

The second floor was as Christopher remembered it: blinding white and drenched in the smell of bleach. He placed a hand over his mouth and nose as he walked.

There were more tables in the hallway this time around, each with stacks of paper weighted down by pill bottles. As ever, Christopher felt the need to read through them, despite knowing they could offer no solace. This place was no hospital; it was a morgue.

Patient No. 284: Room 314. Suffering from severe burns on her face; reconstructive services not required or recommended as patient is resistant to anesthesia. Receives frequent visits from female companion. Please deliver painkillers.

The bottle's contents rattled when Christopher picked it up. He shrugged. It wouldn't have been placed in his path if he hadn't been meant to do something about it. Unlike his first trip down this hallway, when he grabbed the doorknob to room 314 it turned easily and allowed him inside... the big top at Wonderland Amusement Park?

Prima and Terceira were seated at the table with no sign of injury. Thankfully the table was clear of food, though that might mean Christopher was about to be on the menu.

He remained where he was, a hand still on the door that had led him there to make sure it didn't disappear and leave him stranded.

The redheaded woman stood up and walked over to him. He was prepared to jerk back and slam the door shut on her. However, all she did was hold out her hand.

"You've got Terceira's medicine, eh?"

Christopher handed the bottle to her. "I guess so." He paused. "Will it help with anything?"

"Not really, and not for very long."

"The note said that Terceira's face had been burned. Is that why—"

"The veil? Yeah, that's why," Prima snapped. She sighed. "We were taking the country by storm back in those days. Started at the bar where we met. Some jerk decided to get a little too handsy with her and I took him out back to have a 'chat.' Ended up inviting him for dinner when Terceira suggested we hide the body in a bit of an unconventional way. Waste not, want not."

"Then what happened?" Christopher wasn't particularly interested in hearing this, but if he could keep Prima reminiscing then she might not turn on him. He had hoped she might reveal more about Wonderland, but from the sound of it, she didn't have that in mind.

"Love at first sight!" From the table, he could hear Terceira giggling. "We dumped all our money into an RV and took our show cross-country. We kept ourselves well-fed."

Prima looked at her wife with pure admiration. "I couldn't even give you a guess at how many people we killed. Whenever the cops started to catch up, we'd just dump whatever vehicle we had at the time and buy or steal a new one. Had a ton of aliases; my favorite was Scarlet Rettke, and Terceira's was... what was it, again, dearest?"

"Diahara Sanchez," Terceira answered fondly.

"But... why?" Christopher asked. "If the first murder was done to defend Terceira, then why continue killing? I could see going on the run to evade the cops, but adding more murder charges onto that just... doesn't make sense."

"Who ever said we cared about making sense?" Prima laughed. "We did it for the rush, because it was exciting and we enjoyed it. Everyone needs a hobby, Chrissy."

"And then, Los Angeles," Terceira hissed. "I'll admit we got arrogant. We weren't covering our tracks as well as we should have. The cops were incompetent and couldn't pin us down, but someone else was following us." She slammed her fist down on the table. "*That man.* Abel!"

"What? *Abel?* But he's a gardener!"

"And gardeners have access to all kinds of chemicals, don't they?" Prima growled.

Terceira dropped her head. "My beautiful face, ruined!"

Prima hurried to her side. "Darlin', you're still pretty! If only I'd been faster."

"Oh hush, you were brilliant. I'd have died without you."

Christopher took the opportunity to see himself out while Prima was distracted with consoling Terceira. If they noticed him leaving, they didn't try to follow, and he was back in the hallway once more with the door securely closed behind him.

Well, that explains why they killed Abel, Christopher thought. *But not why they're here. What would any of that have to do with Wonderland?*

What had he learned? He already knew that Prima and Terceira were psychopathic murderers.

But the acid attack didn't kill Terceira. Prima saved her, and wasn't hurt by it herself, he realized. *So what* did *kill them?*

He continued down the hall, and it wasn't long before he winced in pain from having bumped into another near-invisible white table. The papers on this one read:

Patients No. 45 and No. 46: Room 315. Please bring antidepressants.

Christopher picked up the bottle which, upon closer examination, had a smiling face on its label. Room 315 was directly to his left. He braced himself for this room before entering Godwin's Deli.

Matthew and Morgan were sitting on opposite ends of the shop. Morgan was staring down at his lap, but Christopher could tell he'd been crying. Matthew was glaring out the window with his arms crossed. The tension set Christopher even more on edge, and he took a moment before speaking.

"Ehm... hello, again?"

Morgan looked up and gave him a small wave. "Hi, Chris. Nice to see you."

"Yeah. Nice," Matthew muttered.

"Mattie, I said I was sorry!"

"That's not good enough!"

Oh, dear. Christopher had been expecting as much. Even if the twins had been on good terms before, they were certain to be feuding after Morgan had killed Matthew. But hadn't Matthew himself been the one to say that dying was the only way out?

"I don't understand. I thought you wanted to die," Christopher offered.

Matthew turned on him. "It's not about that! And it looks like I was wrong about it being an escape, anyway. We're *still* stuck here. Just like always."

"Not about that? What could be worse than killing a per—?"

Christopher was cut off for the second time that hour. "It's about everything *else* Morgan did!" The blue-eyed twin shrank down, getting ready for a verbal assault he had probably heard many times before. "It's his fault that I'm stuck on this island!"

"His fault? How?" Christopher got the feeling he was going to get another life story out of that question. Maybe this one would be more pertinent to his situation.

Matthew didn't disappoint. "When we were adopted, things were great," he answered, though he was still staring directly at Morgan. Christopher got the feeling that Matthew was speaking more to his twin than to him. "We had great parents. Our dads were always there for us, and no one in Wonderland cared that they were gay. But then *Morgan* decided to ruin it. *They were just a little late picking us up, but you couldn't let it go, could you?*"

"I thought they abandoned us!" Morgan snapped. "Can you blame me? Our own mother left us!"

"They weren't her!" Matthew countered. "They apologized. You seem to think that's good enough to forgive you, but I guess it wasn't good enough for them, huh?"

Christopher was worried Matthew might start throwing the salt and pepper shakers on the table at his brother. Instead, the brown-eyed twin faced him. He could feel himself begin to tremble at the look of rage in Matthew's eyes. He needed to find a way to change the subject, and he realized something that might do just that.

"The eye transplant... when did that happen?"

The twins exchanged a glance that wasn't filled with loathing or despair. "What transplant? We were both born with heterochromia."

Morgan placed his finger beneath his left eye. "Blue." And beneath his right eye. "And brown."

Christopher squinted. They were right; their eyes were two different colors. Had they always been that way? He blinked again, and he was sure that Morgan had two blue eyes and Matthew had two brown. He shook his head. A small detail like that didn't matter; he couldn't even quite remember why he'd had the thought. The momentary interlude was broken as Matthew returned to his tirade, preventing Christopher from dwelling on it.

"So anyway, Morgan started causing problems, driving the family apart, and when he was sixteen he ran off. *Without me.* Funny how abandonment issues are only important when they apply to him, isn't it?"

"I sent you postcards!"

"Oh, great, postcards! That really makes watching your parents split up so much better! And with Pop gone, someone needed to stick around and help Dad run the shop. Guess who it was? I'll give you a hint: it was the one who wanted to go to college and see the world. But Morgan's got issues, so I guess that leaves me to clean up the mess. And then Dad died, and there was no way I was ever going to leave. Couldn't let the shop die, too."

"I came back," Morgan said. "I know I messed up, but I came back. I tried to fix it."

"You can't fix it," Matthew spat bitterly. "I needed you to fix it back when this started, and instead you ran away like the coward you are."

Christopher was too uncomfortable not to say anything. He just wanted out of the room. This story wasn't any more helpful than Prima and Terceira's. He held the pill bottle out to Matthew. "So, I have these antidepressants that I'm meant to give you?"

Morgan held his hand up, palm flat. "Toss 'em here."

"And another thing!"

Christopher threw the pills and left before Matthew could launch into another attack. He couldn't say he pitied Morgan too much, but the knowledge that not even death was going to get him off this island sank in once he closed the door. If he didn't find a way to escape, he could be trapped in the hospital with his worst failure tormenting him, too.

At least now he knew he couldn't trust the hospital documents he'd found, though that came as no surprise. Everything about Wonderland had been fabricated from the beginning, and nothing added up. Maybe Bethlem hadn't been some kind of torture chamber, after all. Maybe it was just a regular hospital abandoned after a fire. It wouldn't have been anyone's favorite place, but hospitals rarely were.

Still, the end of the hall was a ways off. Christopher hunched down and felt around in front of him, pleased when he was able to locate the next table without hurting himself.

There weren't many islanders left; this was probably one of the last patients he'd have to check on.

The second his eyes fell on the paper, he was not looking forward to it.

Patients No. 0 and No. 1: Room 316. Please secure with straight jackets. Do not make direct eye contact.

However, there were no straight jackets on the table.

Fantastic.

The room was an eye-gougingly irritating shade of pink. Christopher tried to avoid direct eye contact with the color, but it was everywhere.

"Hello, hello!" Joseph greeted him.

"You're just in time, I've finished frosting the cake!" Mary added with her plastered-on smile.

"Go ahead, have a seat at the table, bud," Joseph said. He moved to guide Christopher into a seat at the pink table, but the young man dodged his massive arms. When Mary opened her mouth to begin her horrendous song, Christopher grabbed the gun from its holster, raising it to show the two that he was not to be messed with. He'd had quite enough of that.

"Well, I never!" Mary clucked.

"No, I don't suppose you have," Christopher said. "But now is not the time for manners. I want answers."

"You're sure you wouldn't rather have a slice of cake?" Joseph said. "It's good. Mary's the best cook."

"Thank you, dear."

"No, I don't want your plastic cake! I want to know what happened to Mickey! Something must have happened to him in this town, and he's trying to tell me but he can't, and it must have something to do with why he came to Woodrow Children's Asylum, because otherwise there would be no reason for me to be here!"

Joseph and Mary stopped smiling, something Christopher was amazed they could even do. They scowled at him, and when they spoke, their cheerful voices were gone.

"You just had to keep picking at the scars, didn't you? You couldn't just leave well enough alone, could you?" Mary started, her voice growing in volume with each word. "Now look what you've done! The perfect world that we created is destroyed, all because of you! It's all your fault that he is the way he is!"

"*Our* son!" Joseph added, his face bright red, veins standing out on his neck and forehead. "Mickey is our son, not yours, but you corrupted him! All day and all night, he just kept going on and on about Christopher Robinson this and Christopher Robinson that. 'I want to go see Christopher,' 'when is Christopher going to visit,' 'I don't love you like I love Christopher!' Do you have any idea how annoying it was? He could have been the perfect child to complete our perfect family in our perfect home, but YOU—!"

Joseph's head twitched so violently to the side that Christopher was certain his neck broke, but it snapped back into place the next second. The same happened with Mary, and with their other limbs, as they continued to scream in unison.

"We were the ones who rescued him from that hovel, we were the ones who took him into our home! Ungrateful *wretch*!"

Christopher noticed that the entire doll collection was present for the affair, staring at them with unfeeling eyes and fake expressions. All but one, whose eyes reflected deep sadness and fear. A doll with hazel eyes and brown hair that wore a yellow sweater and held a stuffed rabbit.

"You did this," Christopher breathed. He took a step toward them, raising the gun and releasing the handle of the door. "It's *your* fault, all of it!"

They lunged, and Christopher pulled the trigger. By luck, the bullet went straight through Mary's head, but there was no blood. The gunshot stunned them, however, and Christopher got a good look at what they really were underneath their charade: two giant dolls with knives for fingers, buttons for eyes, and mouths that opened far wider than they should have been able to, unhinged. They could swallow a child whole, and they'd be able to take a good chunk out of Christopher. Their elbows, knees, and waists could all turn at three hundred and sixty degrees, so Christopher knew trying to dodge around them would do no good.

He panicked and fired every shot he had in rapid succession.

Only a few bullets struck their targets, blasting holes in the plastic to slow the dolls' advance. The other bullets hit the small, inert dolls behind them, at which the Mary and Joseph dolls screeched in anger.

When the gun ran out of bullets, Christopher tossed it aside and reached for the hatchet, and was then faced with the dilemma of how exactly he was going to kill the abominations in front of him. He might be able to chop them up, but it was going to take a lot of time and effort. While he was hacking away at one, he would leave himself exposed to attack from the other.

He reached for the door with one hand, but it was gone. He'd lost it.

Joseph sprang at him, trying to grab him with that grotesquely large mouth. Christopher ducked under the table only to have it be swatted away by Mary.

Think, think! Mickey must want you to defeat them, so there must be a way to do it!

As he dodged Mary's claws, the contrast of dark red on bubblegum pink caught his eye. One of the dolls that he had accidentally shot was bleeding, and its eyes were closed.

Christopher dove between Joseph's legs, not that it mattered. The doll-man simply whirled on his waist joint and shrieked at Christopher as he approached the smaller dolls. Christopher took the knife from his pocket and flipped it open. With the switchblade in one hand and the hatchet in the other, he set about destroying the creepy collection.

Each doll he stabbed bled and let out a cry that was echoed by Joseph and Mary, but killing their life source did not immobilize the two large monsters entirely, and turning his back on them was a huge mistake. One of them—Christopher couldn't see which—lashed out, and four knives raked across his back. He let out a harsh yell and fell into the corpses of the dolls that he had just demolished. He dropped the hatchet and it spun away from his reach.

I'm supposed *to kill them,* he thought weakly. This was different from the plant monster. These were, in some way, children. *I'm supposed to do this. I'm doing the right thing. Mickey, help me.*

Christopher could barely move, but he found the strength to bury himself in the pile of dolls. Those that weren't "dead" resisted his efforts—he could have sworn some of them bit him, scratched him, tried to gouge his eyes out or suffocate him, and dug their stubby fingers into the gashes on his back to make them hurt even more—but he safely covered himself. There was no way Mary and Joseph would attack their own "children" and end up killing themselves in their search for him.

From the semi-safety of the dolls, unable to see the rest of the world, Christopher continued his work, slitting the throats of the dolls with the knife. He had no way of knowing how many he had killed or how many he had left to go, but soon his hands were stained a deep red. Their blood was everywhere; on his hands, underneath his fingernails, in his hair, on his face, and in his mouth and nose.

He listened closely to the screams of Mary and Joseph to determine whether he had succeeded in destroying them yet. Their cacophony of pain was still loud and clear, so he continued to worm his way through the dolls, gasping when he shifted the wrong way or when the pain became too much for him to endure silently.

Their screams ended at last, and Christopher re-emerged from the pile. He did not stand up, but simply looked over his work; a mountain of doll corpses, blood gushing everywhere and staining every inch of carpet and furniture. Joseph and Mary, too, were on the ground. They were bleeding from their mouths, noses, eyes, and a hundred cuts on their bodies, each injury representing a "dead" doll. Mary attempted to rise and strike Christopher when she saw him. Her angry snarl died away in a gurgle of blood, and she was still.

He looked over the pile again, seeking the one doll he had spared. Brown hair, hazel eyes, yellow sweater, stuffed rabbit.

He picked up the doll and brushed its hair. It became heavier in his arms until it was no longer a doll at all. Christopher set the boy down.

Mickey picked up the bag that had fallen away from Christopher when he'd first been slashed, the straps cut cleanly. The boy removed the peroxide and bandages from it. "You're hurt, Christopher. Let me help."

Christopher nodded and removed what was left of his shirt. Mickey doused the bandages in the disinfectant and brushed them against the wounds before wrapping them. Christopher bit his lip to prevent himself from yelping at the sting.

"If this is truly my fault, then please, please forgive me," Christopher said.

"It's more complicated than that," Mickey answered. "I'm not upset with you for what you did. I'm upset because of what you didn't do."

"So you *are* upset with me, then?" Christopher frowned.

Mickey finished bandaging Christopher and pulled something else out of the bag: a white button-up shirt and a blue sweater vest. The orderly decided not to question the appearance of his old clothes and put them on, feeling a little more himself than he had been lately.

When he was done, Mickey answered him. "Yes."

"Is that what you were trying to tell me before? That you were upset with me, and I wouldn't understand if you told me that?"

"More or less, but there's more to it, and you wouldn't understand because there's so much that you don't know. I could never have told you why I was upset before this; you wouldn't have believed it. But now that you've been here, you can see it. I'm upset because you didn't save me from this."

Christopher sighed. He still didn't understand the situation, but he turned and hugged Mickey. "I'm sorry. I would have, if I'd been able to."

Mickey grabbed Christopher's hand. "Just come with me. It will make more sense soon enough."

They left the pink room, traveling down the hall to Room 317.

*L*ike the other rooms, Room 317 contained much more than the standard furniture within a few square feet. When Christopher and Mickey stepped through the doorway, they found themselves back in Woodrow Children's Asylum.

Far from feeling relieved to be home, Christopher looked around as if something might leap out of the shadows at any moment. For once, no danger presented itself. That was no cause for celebration. He was certain they were nowhere near the true asylum, and this was an illusion conjured by the island to lure him into a false sense of security before springing another horror upon him.

Rather than disappear again, Mickey stayed right at his side. Frustration and impatience emanated from his every movement, but he didn't let go of Christopher's hand.

"You know where we have to go," he said.

Christopher nodded. "And what's going to be waiting for me there?"

"I think you know."

The orderly sighed. He had an idea, he just didn't want it to be true.

They walked through the West Wing together. The sounds of children laughing and crying resonated from the opposite end of the asylum, but Christopher resolved not to go check on the others. They were probably figments of his imagination anyway, as Mickey wasn't bothered by the noises in the slightest. For all Christopher knew, the rest of the asylum might be completely silent, and he was having an auditory hallucination. Or maybe there were monsters waiting behind the doors in the East Wing.

It wasn't as if the other children were important right now, anyway. All that really mattered was the room at the end of the hall, and the two reached it with no disruptions.

Christopher hesitated when his fingers touched the doorknob. As much as he wanted this ordeal to be over, he didn't want to go in and have his suspicions confirmed.

Mickey placed a hand over Christopher's. "You have to go inside."

"I know." He shook his head. "But, before I do, I want to apologize for upsetting you. You know I would never do something to make you sad on purpose."

The boy tilted his head. "Yes, I'm sure that you would never intentionally cause anyone grief. However, the fact remains that you did, and you have to atone for it either way."

Christopher grinned at him. "When did you get such a big vocabulary?"

"You'll understand soon. Are you ready?"

"As ready as I'll ever be," he replied. Together they turned the door knob and stepped into the true Room 317.

"Hello, Christopher."

"Hello, Michael."

Michael was sitting on the bed, just as he had done all those years ago. His hazel eyes still had that same too-clever glint that shone from beneath messy, dead-leaf brown hair. They gained a malicious gleam as he smirked at Christopher.

"You didn't bring me any food this time. What kind of caretaker are you?"

"Don't antagonize him," Mickey said, frowning. He folded his arms. "You've done quite enough of that already."

Christopher looked back and forth between the two of them, trying to reconcile their existence in his mind. It was obvious now that Michael was a grown-up Mickey, but how could they *both* be in the same place at the same time?

The smaller of the brunets sensed his distress and patted his hand. "I promise, it will all make... *relative* sense."

"Not that it even matters if we try to explain it to you." Michael shrugged. "You're going to forget. Just like you forgot me."

"Forgot *me*, you mean," Mickey snapped. "Whose fault is it that he forgets?"

"And leaving him a tortured mess is so much better?"

"He wouldn't *be* a tortured mess if you would—"

"Enough!" Christopher cut in. "We are all going to calm down and talk about this. *Nicely.* So you," he jabbed a finger at Michael, "be quiet for a minute. You'll get your turn to speak soon."

Michael's expression darkened. "You're going to tell me what to do? *You're* going to tell *me* what to do?"

"He just did," Mickey spat. "And I think that means it's my turn to talk."

The older of the two glared at the younger, but kept his mouth shut. Mickey faced Christopher and gave him a small smile. "This must be very confusing to you, and I'm sorry for that. I'll try to explain things as best I can.

"To start with, Michael and I are two sides of the same person. I am the more logical side, the one that can actually reason my way through my emotions and not throw a massive fit over every little thing. In other words, I'm the one you knew at the asylum, the one you raised. You did a good job, and if you had stayed with me until I became an adult, things might have ended differently. But you didn't, and this is how things are."

"What do you mean, I didn't?" Christopher asked. A strange ache began to form at the back of his skull, creeping down to his arms and chest with every heartbeat.

"I was adopted," Mickey answered. "By Mary and Joseph, of course. It was all rushed along; I imagine they paid Madam Margot rather well to keep some things off the records. One day I was at the asylum, and the next I was brought to Wonderland. You promised that you would write, or visit, that we'd see each other again soon. That never happened. I believed in you and I held on to the hope that you would come for me, no matter what Mary and Joseph did to me.

"I'm sure you can imagine the kind of parents that they were. They didn't want to actually take care of a child as much as they wanted a doll that could walk and talk on its own, and then only when *they* wanted it to. A mindless thing that would parrot its affection for them day in and day out and never cause problems. The kind of child that can never exist.

"Joseph was away all the time on business, so I didn't have to deal with him too often. But Mary—she was the real problem. Every time he went out of town she'd drink away her sorrows, and she was a mean drunk. Violent. I guess her reasoning was that if she couldn't break me mentally, she'd break me physically."

Mickey paused when Christopher brought him into a hug and whispered a quiet apology. Michael stood, that cold sneer on his face once more. "But things only got worse from there! And this is where I come into the story."

"I'm not done yet," Mickey retorted.

"I think you are. And it's only my ideas that matter here. You can prattle on about how 'logical' you are, but the fact of the matter is that logic and reason don't have any power on this island. *I* do."

Michael grabbed Christopher's shoulders and ended the embrace by shoving him against the wall, leaving Mickey with his arms outstretched toward empty air.

"Enjoying the sob story so far? The kid might be acting nice to get you on his side, but he hates you just as much as I do."

"I don't believe you," Christopher replied. "Even if you're grown up now, you're still Mickey to me."

"Hah!" Michael pressed his forearm against his former caretaker's neck. "Still Mickey? Was I still Mickey at the police station, when you wouldn't let me out of the cell? Or at the deli, where you were *so* eager to get away from me?" He lowered his voice to a whisper. "How about at the bar, or afterwards? Was I still Mickey then?"

Christopher's stomach turned and Michael let him go.

"*My* story begins after one of Mary's beatings, when she dislocated one of my shoulders. I had to go to the hospital to get it fixed. And, wouldn't you know it, they just left me there. Well..." His smile took on a resemblance to a kicked dog baring its teeth. "No, it was way worse than that. If they had just left me there, then I could have walked back to their house, maybe run away altogether like Morgan did. But, no. It would be much more accurate to say that they *sold* me.

"The others you encountered on the island all had family and loved ones who would have come looking for them if they went missing. But I didn't, since you obviously weren't coming to save me after years of abandonment. I doubt I so much as crossed your mind once I was out of Woodrow. So I stayed at the hospital, and Mary and Joseph probably told anyone who asked—and I'm sure not many people did—that they'd sent me off to foster care or something. I was just too much of a problem child for them to handle, or some other nonsense.

"Once the doctors knew no one was coming for me, they started their experiments. I wasn't the only one, of course. Anyone they found who was alone became one of their test subjects. They passed the third floor off as a mental ward, but we all knew better than to think they were actually trying to help us." He was shaking now. "Sleep deprivation, removing sensory nerves, nerve gas, psychoactive drugs, exposure to radiation, even experimenting with our blood and hormone levels. A lot of the subjects didn't survive, but they always had ways of finding more."

Christopher moved to give Michael a hug too, but the other shot him a glare that kept him rooted to the spot. "I was tortured for over a year in that place. I played the role of the good test subject, I took all my pills without complaint, I didn't fight back when they gave me shots, I didn't try to murder anyone. One thing Mary and Joseph did teach me was how to keep quiet and survive. So I did, and I waited, and the longer I waited the more I became aware that I was even more different from normal people than the other patients. I could do things with my mind that they couldn't. Maybe it was an ability I'd always had, or maybe whatever the doctors were trying to do actually worked.

"I started off by practicing on some of the other test subjects when the doctors weren't around. At first it was just little, easy things—making someone tired, making someone laugh. The more I practiced, the more I could make them do. Hormones and chemicals are interesting things. If you mess around with them a little you can get people to do whatever you want, and they'll think it was all of their own accord. Of course, it doesn't work all the time, and it helps if someone's already a little addled or inebriated. Sound familiar, Chris?

"When it came down to it, psychic powers weren't what got me out. I knew I couldn't control the minds of the entire hospital staff at once. I escaped using plain old violence, and then I set the place on fire and disappeared into the woods." His smirk widened. "But I can't take all the credit for that idea."

"I had to cover my tracks," Mickey said coolly. "Unfortunately the structural damage meant there could be no thorough investigation of the third floor, so those experiments were never brought to light. By that point, all the doctors who performed them had been stabbed to death, so I accepted that as retribution."

"What?" Christopher stared at Mickey. "*You* caused the hospital fire?"

Mickey stared down at his feet. "I told you, we're two sides of the same person, more or less. It was the logical thing to do."

"Which means he's a killer, too," Michael chuckled. "And not just the hospital. The school, as well. Lots of schools. And I stabbed a lot more people to death along the way. So which of us is worse, Christopher Robinson? Your sweet little arsonist, who killed dozens of people at a time, or the creepy man with a knife who picked people off one by one? Which one can you forgive?"

"I–I don't know," Christopher answered.

"Maybe you'd like to know more about the people we killed before you decide," Michael went on. "Mary and Joseph were first. Had to take them out, for what they'd done. They were more monstrous than I was. They didn't even move the key, and they were so surprised to see me, so sure I'd died in the hospital fire, that it didn't take much to overpower and stab them to death."

Christopher shook his head. "That's enough, now! I don't want to hear more!"

Michael went on anyway. "Then I went for Morgan. There was so little gossip to be had in Wonderland that even stories from years ago lingered. I heard all about him when I was a kid on the island, how he'd had a loving family and had thrown it away for nothing. And when he came back to be the town sheriff, he harassed me constantly. Guess I gave off that 'juvenile delinquent' vibe. He never once tried to get to the bottom of where all my bruises came from or help me in any way, it was always just 'why aren't you in class, Michael' and 'why are you out after curfew, Michael.' I hated him.

"But, as luck would have it, I accidentally killed Matthew instead. It was dark and I was never any good at telling them apart. Morgan came in just as I finished Matthew off, and I fixed my mistake. No wonder why he's so mad at Morgan, huh? If it weren't for him, Matthew would have lived to whatever ripe old age suicidal people usually reach."

Christopher swallowed hard, even though his mouth was dry. He couldn't help thinking about the twins' corpses in the deli. Had they looked that way when Michael had killed them, too?

"Prima and Terceira didn't come until later," Mickey said, and Christopher cringed. He didn't want to imagine the child having any part in this. Hearing him talk about it just confirmed that he really had been involved in the gruesome deaths of multiple people. Christopher couldn't bear it. "After I killed the people who had wronged me, I burned down Woodrow Children's Asylum. Don't worry—you weren't there. I checked."

Michael folded his arms. "I would have murdered you myself if you were. Good job getting yourself out in time."

Mickey leered at his older counterpart for that comment, but continued: "I didn't have much direction after I burned down the asylum. I was so angry at the world that it didn't matter who I killed, as long as someone suffered. It took time for me to become as feared as Prima and Terceira, but I became known for my alternating methods of stabbing lone strangers and burning down schools and hospitals."

"The Slash-and-Burn Killer. A pretty decent title, if I do say so myself," Michael added. "I got around to Prima and Terceira after I thought I'd have half a chance of surviving an encounter with them. If they hadn't been tired out they might have gotten the upper hand, and even then they were difficult to handle. But I showed up at just the right time and managed to kill them both.

"I had a few more good years after that. I lost track of my body count. Last I remember, it was getting close to three hundred. But eventually, all fun must come to an end. The cops finally caught up to me on a very special day: March seventeenth, 1984. Of course I wasn't going to just let them take me in. I shot myself." He put two fingers to his left temple, then flicked his hand away. His eye turned bloodshot and horrible black lines extended from the point of imaginary impact, stretching across the left side of his face. Christopher stared in revulsion and recognition of that eye. "Just like that."

"Then I woke up here," Mickey said. "On the island I hated, surrounded by the people I killed."

"Then this *is* the afterlife?" Christopher asked, still taking it in. "But what am I doing here? I thought you said you didn't kill me...?"

"No. I never found you," Mickey said. "You weren't at the asylum, and I didn't find any record of you anywhere else. You disappeared."

"Just like before," Michael growled. "You really have a knack for avoiding me. It might not have even been too late at that point. You could have talked some of that oh-so-precious sense into my logical half, even if you didn't have much of it yourself. But it's far too late for that now."

"I don't understand. Why am I here?"

Michael's grin grew even wider, causing more cracks to appear along his face. "Should I tell him?"

"I don't see any reason not to at this point," Mickey replied with a shrug. Christopher was almost pleased that they had stopped bickering, but the fact that their uniting factor was their anger toward him destroyed any chance of his feeling accomplished.

The older side of the killer looped an arm around Christopher's shoulders and drew him in close. Too close. Christopher was getting a far closer look at Michael's broken eye than he'd ever wanted. He struggled against the hold, but it was no use. He was too tired, and Michael was too strong.

"Oh, Christopher. Dear, gentle, stupid Christopher. You're here because you aren't real. No one here is, except the half-pint and me. You're all just made up, by us, to torture ourselves! Isn't that a hoot? It just keeps getting *funnier and funnier* every time I say it!" Michael let Christopher go, breaking off into a fit of manic laughter.

"Not real? But that's—"

"Insane? Well, I guess now we know that you *do* think I'm crazy. That hurts a little bit, even if you are right."

"Calm down," Mickey sighed.

"None of this makes any kind of sense," Christopher groaned. "You say I'm not real, but how could I be here if I wasn't?"

"You asked if this was the afterlife. In a way, it is," Mickey said. "This is my afterlife. My punishment. I've tried to leave this place, so many times, and I can't. The bridge is out, and anything you even try to float across the lake sinks immediately or gets eaten. I'm trapped here forever. It's what I deserve. But as for you, Christopher, that's where things get even more complicated. You weren't here from the beginning."

"It's not complicated at all," Michael replied. "The island pulled him out of my memories to upset me once the others stopped being effective."

"I wasn't here? What do you mean?" If Christopher hadn't always been there, maybe there was a way out, after all.

"Everyone else on this island has always been here. You're the only one who comes from the outside, and in the earliest days, you didn't come at all," Mickey explained. "It was only after I'd started to get a sense of how the island works that you showed up one day, disoriented and looking for me. I was able to trace you back to a piece of Woodrow that was connected to the island, another part of the illusion. You always wake up there and come here, following me."

"I was actually glad to see you at first," Michael hissed. "I thought after all that time, you had finally come to save me. That's probably why this island set you up the way it did. But you didn't even recognize me! You only wanted him, the 'innocent' one. You couldn't have cared less about me, just like you couldn't have cared less when I was alive!"

"I'm sure there's more to it than that. This is Christopher, after all," Mickey retorted.

"No, it isn't. It's just a cheap copy made up to toy with me by whatever sent me here."

Christopher rubbed his forehead. "Let me get this straight. This whole island, and Woodrow, are just illusions created by your mind, to punish you for murdering people? And you're actually dead, along with everyone else, except me?"

"Technically no one else can be dead, since they were never alive to begin with. The people on the island are made out of my memories of them," Mickey corrected. "That would mean you, too, Christopher. You aren't alive, and you never were."

"I'm the only real person here," said Michael, "stuck with myself and everyone I hate until the end of time."

A loud meow sounded from the corner of the room, and the deformed tuxedo cat moved out of the shadows. Cheshire wound around Christopher's legs with a purr.

"And the cat?" he barely dared to ask.

"The *cat*," Michael barked. A swift movement with one leg brought the beast away from Christopher, and then he kicked it hard. It struck one of the bedposts and screeched.

Michael started after it, but Christopher grabbed his arm. "Stop that!"

"Or *what?*" Michael shouted, pushing Christopher off. "You don't understand anything about this place. That cat has been watching me ever since I got here. Just watching! I never killed it, never even *saw* it. It's just here watching me!"

Mickey helped Christopher up. "I have a theory that whatever sent me here is using the cat to keep an eye on me, and to help you when it can."

"Why bother, if I'm not real?" Christopher asked bitterly.

"Because it sent you," Michael answered. "It is the island. It is what keeps me trapped here and makes me suffer, and it wants me to keep suffering. What better way can you think of to do that than dangling you in front of me, knowing I can never go back to the way things were? But it made one big mistake in its calculations. I like watching you suffer. I like it a *lot*. And you coming here did *something* to the island that makes it possible to enjoy it again and again. Every time you die, everything resets back to the way it was before you came, so we can just keep doing this for the rest of time!"

"But I don't want that," Mickey said. "I am angry at you, Christopher. I still feel hurt and betrayed that you never came to save me, or even wrote to me, and it frustrates me to no end that you never understand what I try to tell you. But I also still love you, and I won't let him hurt you. Eventually, some way, I'll convince you to listen to me and not leave the asylum."

"Like you can do anything to stop me! Logic, reason, that won't get you anywhere here. This place runs on emotion. Fear, hatred, despair—all the things I excel at. That's why *you* still look like a child, while I get to be in my real body. I'm in charge, I make the rules of this game, and there isn't a thing you can do to protect him or anyone else."

Mickey quieted, and for the first time Christopher noticed that he looked afraid of his other half. They might have been the same person originally, but he couldn't bring himself to believe that they were the same person now. They clearly had different ideas and feelings, and whatever Michael was talking about, Mickey was terrified of it.

That fear only encouraged Michael.

"You see, Christopher..." Michael removed a knife from his pants pocket. Mickey darted between the two adults, but Michael tossed him aside easily, once again pinning Christopher to the wall with the knife ready. "I'm going to kill you now. Then you're going to wake up in Woodrow, without any idea that any of this happened, and you're going to do it all over again, just like always. You might make a few different decisions. I might add or remove some monsters from your path. But you will always end up in this room, unable to save me or yourself. I will drive you insane, kill you, and love every minute of it."

"Don't!" Mickey cried.

Michael rammed the blade into Christopher's stomach and twisted it. Christopher gasped—every other wound that he had suffered, even the Jabberwock's poison, was nothing compared to this. Those had all just been imaginings of pain; the knife wound was very real.

Mickey got up and pulled Michael's arm back. The knife came out of Christopher's stomach. A thin line of blood splattered on the floor. "Stop it!"

It took no effort for Michael to knock him away, and Mickey stumbled and fell. "I'd tell you to make me, but I've already established that you can't. You're just as weak as he is, and eventually I'll find a way to get rid of you."

"Listen to me next time, Christopher," Mickey said quietly. "Listen and do what I tell you, don't leave me behind, and maybe this won't happen again. *Please*."

Even from his position against the wall, through the pain and the feeble efforts he was making to keep pressure on the knife wound, Christopher knew that Mickey was about to cry. He tried to go and comfort the small boy, but the second he took a step away from the wall, he fell to the ground.

"Are you serious?" Michael stood over him, and Christopher felt sure a kick was coming. "Are you being serious right now? The kid confessed that he's a murderer, that we're the same person, and that you're here to suffer for it. And you're *still* trying to get to him?" The anticipated kick arrived, knocking what little wind Christopher had recovered back out of him. "Where was any of that when I was alive? When it would have made a difference? Where were you when I needed you?!"

"S-sorry..."

Rather than placate him, the apology only caused Michael to bring the knife down again with even more fury than the first stab. Christopher coughed, and a worrisome amount of blood came out of his mouth.

"God, I hate you."

The knife came out, and by no means was it done cleanly. The next attack was higher up, piercing Christopher's chest.

"I hate you so much! And I'll *always* hate you. I don't care if I am trapped here forever, as long as I get to see you suffer, it's worth it. This world is a dream come true for me!"

"S-s..." There was too much blood being lost—and too much of it bubbling through Christopher's throat—for him to say anything.

Mickey watched in terror some feet away as Michael continued to cut Christopher open, coating them both in blood, and his crying face was one of the last things Christopher saw before his vision faded to black. The final sight that his eyes would behold was the single amber eye of the grinning cat that was sitting underneath the bed.

He could feel his memories drifting away as he lay there, everything being erased in preparation for another round of this "game." It was a curious feeling; he knew he ought to remember something, yet he couldn't for the life of him think what it might be. Soon he had lost enough of his memories to not feel worried about it anymore—or perhaps that was only the blood loss going to his head.

What blood loss?

Christopher drifted off, unsure of whether he was dying or simply falling asleep, and unsure why he even thought he'd be dying, anyway. What he did know was that he would wake soon, promptly put this strange feeling behind him, and attend to the children at the asylum, as he always did and always would.

Appearances can be deceiving, but sometimes a quick glance can be all one needs to see something's true nature.

If one were to look at the wreckage of Woodrow Children's Asylum, the overall impression would be one of despair. The old brick building was charred and falling apart, and the surrounding area had never grown back from the fire that had ravaged it twenty years prior. Birds did not fly over it, and no creature would cross it to get from one end of the forest to the other.

Woodrow itself fared no better, having been officially declared a ghost town not long after the fire. It was erased from maps, the roads leading to it were closed, and it was by and large forgotten until the disappearances began. Groups of thrill-seeking teenagers would make the trek through the woods to the town on weekend trips, and the bravest would even go to the asylum to see how long they could last. Those who dared to stay overnight were never heard from again, and when the survivors were questioned by the police, they would remark that they really couldn't remember if they'd ever heard of the town before that weekend. It was something that had appeared in their subconscious, like a dream they could all very vaguely recall.

Most of the vanishings were simply attributed to the structural unsoundness of the building and town, which was said to attract all manner of dangerous wildlife, even if no one ever saw any such beasts around the place. The investigators who were called in to search the building never found any bodies.

The reports that they did make about the asylum were seldom taken seriously. After all, the area was deserted. The sounds of laughter and the feeling of being watched by a large, bloodshot eye that the search teams spoke of could only be hallucinations, and nothing more.

The fact that those men and women would complain of horrific nightmares shortly after was never looked into seriously.

The suicides that soon followed were swept under the rug.

No one wanted to consider that something as silly as a few nightmares had driven once perfectly stable people to end their lives.

After all, dreams are not real. Dreams cannot hurt you.

As long as you're awake, that is. And, try as you might, you will eventually fall asleep. I may not show up the first night. I may not show up a year from now. But, rest assured if you can, the Dream Man will be coming for you, too.

Until then...

Sleep well.